I0682719

# Storms of Passion

## by

## Lori Power

**Storms of Passion**

Cover Art by *Angela Anderson*

The Wild Rose Press, Inc.
PO Box 708
Adams Basin, NY 14410-0708
Visit us at www.thewildrosepress.com

Publishing History
First Champagne Rose Edition, 2013
Print ISBN 978-1-62830-188-5
Digital ISBN 978-1-62830-189-2

Published in the United States of America

**Someone was singing down on the beach.**

He followed the sound of the female voice.

The identity of the singer couldn't be anyone he knew. Surly no one from town would perch below his parent's house to sing pop music off key. Curious, he strode to the end of the lawn and glanced over the edge, where grass turned to a rocky ledge leading to the beach. He did a double-take at the vision of the woman from the airport. That was her, no doubt about it.

There was no mistaking that long neck and the inky-black hair even more spiky than earlier today. Lowering his glasses down his nose, Tuck watched as she stretched her legs in front of her, crossing her feet at the ankles. What lovely long legs she had. She leaned back as the sun kissed her smooth skin. His fingers ached, watching her weave her fingers through her cropped hair and rubbing the sweat soaked layers from her skin. Supporting her position with one hand behind her back, she continued to lounge on the rock, as if the beach was her living room. Her head bobbed as she sang. Her feet swayed across the sand.

Tuck looked right and left. She's tonight's main attraction and she doesn't even know it. She obviously didn't realize how close the houses were to the beach, and that there was no such thing as privacy in a small town.

He recognized the song as she continued to sing, slightly off key, and he wondered if she'd give voice to the explicit parts of the song as well.

He smiled, nodding his head, completely amused. There was no doubt in his mind now, this had to be the elusive Vivian. Vivacious Vivian. The name absolutely suited her.

# Dedication

T-Love is our adventure together

Chapter One

*His hand, such a sweet caress, leisurely cupped her breast as they spooned for the last warm snuggle on a chilly winter morning. Under her thin camisole, his thumb flitted across her nipple causing it to harden and respond. She awoke to his gentle, but insistent movements over her warm body. Her body heat rose and her heart beat quicken.*

*He stirred behind her and rubbed his loins ever so gently across her backside, prompting her to prostrate into him in a slow circular motion, inviting him in for more. As his hardened member slid along her buttocks, his fingers tickled across her stomach toward its inevitable destination—the wet cleft between her thighs. Moist, warm, and ready, she parted her legs just enough to allow him access as he slid his fingers along her slit, enjoying the slippery feel of the folds envelop his fingers as he slowly massaged and explored her private depths.*

"Whew." Vivian's toes curled in their thick, woolen socks. She stretched them toward the fireplace on this freezing January evening. She glanced up from the manuscript submission she was reading, titled, The Marriage Bed, one of many she hoped to get through

1

this weekend. She focused on the fire's dancing flames before taking her red pen to make some notes in the margin. *Vivid description, but not the right genre for our publishing house.*

Vivian was a reader and loved her job. The publishing house she worked for received a multitude of manuscript submissions on a consistent basis. Some were good, most worthy, and others a pity. Only a few, representing the exceptional, were published. Vivian learned quickly that publishing is big business and expensive. Every manuscript of an unknown author is a complete gamble on how well the book would perform in the marketplace. However, every once in a while, Vivian found a gem. When she found the right combination that would work for the marketplace, it became the most exciting process for all parties concerned. The first time author's bliss of finally being recognized and the publishing house's gamble paying off. The marketing, the movie rights if the manuscript fit the artistic flair of the day, and on and on. For Vivian, who was at the beginning of the process, her reward consisted of the finder's fees for being the one to discover the diamond in the rough.

To some, her job may seem tedious, but to Vivian, being the first line of contact for authors was most pleasurable. Imagine being the reader who launched Jane Austen. Vivian couldn't imagine a better job than reading for a living. Being a reader not only paid the bills, it allowed her to support her other passions of cooking and collecting junk. Well, some may call her treasures junk, but she preferred to think of them as diamonds in the rough.

Sure, she had to sift through a lot of sand to reach

gold. This would apply to both her passions of reading and searching for finds at garage sales, but even in the sand there were quartz and other interesting rocks to keep a miner interested.

She read a bit more of the erotic manuscript that had been slipped onto her romance genre pile. The story was still worth reading and interesting enough. Granted, it was a bit too over the top for their readership of the twenty eight to forty five female, typically busy moms who wanted to lose themselves in an adventure romance, but not over the top that they felt like they were cheating on their spouses. Oh, to discover a Nora Roberts or a Susan Robards, or a Tiffany cut diamond ring! Vivian's career would be made.

She continued to read.

*Awake now, with heat radiating from her core to create a glorious sizzle throughout her nerve endings, she reached behind her to pull his head into the curve of her neck, luxuriating in the feel of his tongue flicking over her rapid pulse. His hand between her legs seemed to keep the same rhythm as her heart beat. She pushed her bottom toward his enlarged member, relishing the feel of its sleek firmness between her buttocks as his hand...*

Vivian stuffed the manuscript pages back in the envelope. "Oh, my God," she said, placing the envelope to the side. *Wow*. Her body filled with warmth. "That's it for that one."

Taking her big, wooly socks off her feet, she pushed out of the comfy, plush chair. Striding toward the kitchen, barefoot, she spotted her sixty-five pound dog lying on his back. He was asleep and his feet were bent in all directions. Snickerdoodle jumped up from his slumber as she reached for her tea cup. Tail wagging, he followed her, she knew in hopes for a treat along the way.

Snickerdoodle was a Golden Doodle, a cross between a Golden Retriever and a full-sized poodle. When she saw him as a twelve week old pup, Snickerdoodle, like the cookie, was the first name that came to her and the name stuck.

Stopping to glance out the window, she touched the small frost lace gathering at the bottom to highlight just how cold the temperature was outside. Reflecting on the first few pages of the steamy manuscript, Vivian contemplated her lack of marriage bed, both the lack of a ring on her forth finger and the passion under the sheets. At thirty-one, she had friends who were male and boyfriends who turned into lovers over the years, but none were her ideal soul mate—that special fit she read about all the time. *People wouldn't write about love, desire, romance, if it didn't exist, right?*

Just after her breakup with her ex-boyfriend, Mark, she started thinking about *real* love. Their breakup had been bad. They dated for more than a year after meeting at a book launch. He owned an electronic bookstore. In this web-based era, Mark had capitalized early on the digital technology of electronic books and created a fortune five-hundred company helping to revitalize the industry which, at the time, had been fledging on how to approach the new age. Mark appeared, to their mutual friends, to be her ideal man. Athletic *and* intelligent, he was well versed on many subjects and seemed completely genuine. *Seemed* being the operative word.

They had been discussing the option of moving in together, the obvious next step in their relationship. In hindsight, perhaps it was those discernible next steps that threatened her sense of independence. Mark wanted Vivian to move into his place and she wanted him to move into hers.

They were having what was supposed to be a romantic dinner at Lindies when the subject of moving in together came up. The tranquil, mood-lit interior contrasted rather significantly with Mark's table manners. Elbows spread on the table, he jabbed and cut his food as though he were a sword fighter, slaughtering the steak. Skewering the overly large piece of meat, he proceeded to scoop potatoes on top as one helping on his fork as if this was the first time he had eaten in weeks, instead of just a few hours.

He glanced around the posh downtown restaurant interior. "Moving to your place doesn't make sense. I work downtown. I'm needed downtown. I live downtown. You can work and do whatever it is you do, anywhere."

Vivian remembered how he made that statement as though he didn't know what she did for a living.

He continued. "All you do is stop by the office once a week to pick up and drop off. You live in the middle of nowhere. The commute alone would be a killer for me fighting traffic from your place."

She remembered how he had lifted the large, green napkin from his lap and scrubbed it across his face, then down over his chin before laying out his terms. He addressed the situation like a business meeting. He laid out the plan as if expecting her to make notes. His vague reference to her profession as the *whatever you do* should have been Vivian's tip-off. She remembered starring into Mark's intent blue gaze. What he had said made sense, to a point. What he failed to take into account was the Brick 'n Brack Shop and Café she opened seasonally. Her shop stood along the edge of her property across from a lovely bed and breakfast. She loved her small side-business where she sold trinkets, and cooked and prepared her favorite dishes. She didn't do this for profit, but for pleasure, and for the seasonal tourists heading to the mountains. The fact that her business actually turned a profit was a reflection of her passion.

Besides, she couldn't move to the busy city. Snickerdoodle needed space to run and be the dog that he is. And she loved her home. Her house was so cozy, warm, inviting, and filled with treasures accumulated over the years, each one holding a memory. Mark was wrong. Her house wasn't in the middle of nowhere. It just wasn't downtown.

As she stood at the window, watching the icicles drip from the branches of the trees in her large back yard, she knew why moving in with Mark wasn't in her best interest, and she noted with some degree of irony, the whole argument was a moot point now anyway.

Her reflections did nothing to change the current situation. She and Mark were no more. All of these thoughts, these imaginary discussions, should have been said back then. She should have made her feelings about her home, her business, her basic wants known to him at the time, but she didn't and she had to own that. She had wanted to make their relationship work— wanted the ideal love. The *love* she shared with Mark was only gloss on the outside.

Running her finger along the cold window, tracing a heart on the misted surface, she *now* knew she never loved Mark. Not truly. But she had wanted to be in love so badly, she had been afraid to look deeper than the surface.

Vivian shook her head, remembering the final confrontation. Her best friend, Marcy, happily married with a toddler and one in the oven, had told her how good Mark was for Vivian—how she shone when Mark was around.

Marcy's pert mouth was set in a determined mold. "Listen girlfriend, we can't have everything our own way. You're an independent woman, I get that. But at some point you're going to need someone to share a life with and in doing so, you have to be willing to compromise a little."

Marcy's stance was almost aggressive, but Vivian understood her best friend only wanted to get her point across, which was for Vivian to be happily settled as she was, all a glow with her most recent pregnancy. Marcy was one of those women who made maternity wear look good, her dressing hugging all the right curves to accentuate the roundness of her burgeoning bulge.

After her visit with Marcy, Vivian had made the decision to move in with Mark, and was eager to celebrate with him. As she eagerly jumped behind the wheel of her Ford Mustang, she planned the menu of the romantic dinner she'd make for them to share, and tell him her decision over a glass of champagne. Yes, he'd like that, she had thought at the time. In her fantasy, they would then make passionate love and he'd ask her to marry him.

She had stopped at the corner deli across from Mark's building to pick out all of his favorites, and then made her way to his penthouse apartment, grocery bags in tow. Before inserting the key, she smiled. She'd tell him he was right about the move after they made love. Grudgingly, she admitted his apartment had more living space than her two-story, cozy cottage. Snicker would adapt. All pets do.

Vivian had let herself in Mark's apartment and walked to the kitchen. She was unpacking the groceries into the fridge when she noticed an open wine bottle on the counter. Strange, maybe he left it there last night? Reaching to cork the bottle, the unmistakable sounds of a couple making love pierced her hearing as a hot knife through butter. The heavy male sighs, the breathy gasps, unmistakable female.

Even though Mark's betrayal occurred nearly nine months previous, the wound still tore at her heart. A tear slid slowly down her cheek as she gazed out to the frozen landscape.

To her credit, she did not do as the books and movies so typically depicted. She didn't storm to the bedroom to confront Mark and his lover. She didn't grandstand. Instead, she'd left the one bag of groceries unpacked on the counter, pulled a sticky note from the drawer, and wrote, *Came by to surprise you with supper, but I was the one surprised. Have a good life. V.* Then, she left.

Her friends had rallied around her, equally shocked and constantly questioning if she was sure there was another woman, when she didn't actually *see* the event. Vivian always just shrugged.

"Why doesn't he call?" she had asked Marcy,

unconvinced. "If I'm wrong about what was going on in his bedroom, then I'm happy to be wrong. So, why hasn't he called to plead his innocence?"

Vivian had waited by the phone. God, how she waited. Time seemed to slow as she served out her sentence in purgatory. She picked up the receiver more times than she could count to listen to the dial tone, ensuring the phone was indeed working. She even went as far as to punch in his number before promptly hanging up.

"Honey, he's likely as hurt and confused as you," Marcy said, but the light of conviction didn't shine in her soft, brown eyes. "I really liked Mark and I liked the two of you together. I want you to be sure about what happened before you throw in the towel."

He never called and within a month, rumors circulated that Mark's new lover had moved in with him. Everyone in the small world of publishing would now see that Mark and his new girlfriend were a couple.

Vivian avoided the office. She was humiliated. To show her face made her sick that she'd be seen as the laughing stock of office gossip. She questioned her relationship with Mark. Did he look elsewhere when she was unmotivated to make the commitment he wanted? Was his infidelity was her fault? Her mother would say so. Keeping a man happy and satisfied should be a woman's top priority, is what her mother would say.

Then the letter arrived.

*Vivian, I am not going to bother to call to explain myself. What happened has happened and is, in my opinion, for the best. I simply want closure as I move on with my life. I don't need to explain or justify my behavior to someone who has her head so far in the clouds she can't see life happening around her. I want to share a life, live life. I don't think any male can live up to your ideal man. I gave up trying. Mark*

Her tears had splattered the surface of the heavy parchment, leaving water blotches and running the ink. Later, when the irony of the letter struck, her eyes were stinging and dry from crying as she crumpled the letter and threw the balled parchment across her bedroom floor.

"That would have been good to know prior to your sleeping with someone else, you bastard!" She yelled at an imaginary Mark into the air of her empty house. "You bastard!"

She wanted to smash furniture, make a big dramatic show of her emotions, but who would care. There was no one to see. No one to care. Empty. That is how Mark's letter had made her feel. He had worded the letter purposely with malicious intent. He wanted her to feel hollow with lost hopes and dreams.

Despite the acknowledgment that they did not truly love one another, the way the relationship ended still spiraled her thoughts. Mark's note, so succinctly written with the minimum amount of words, had been so harsh, she wondered if her *head in the clouds* part was true. Had she created a life where no one could live up to her ideal man?

How could an author be motivated to write about love, passion, and adventure, if it didn't exist? She shook her head. "If romance is out there Snicker, I will certainly find it." She made a vow to the over-sized dog, and bent to give his ears a good scratch.

Vivian opened the back door leading off the kitchen. A blast of frigid cold air sailed over her bare feet, bringing her back to the present. She crossed one foot over the other to preserve their warmth. Vivian waved her hand forward, an indicator for Snicker to go outside do his business. "You go on now." She couldn't help but smile when she glanced down at Snicker. If dogs could talk, she was pretty sure his return stare would be vocalized as, "You try to pee in that cold. I'd rather hold it than freeze my…"

She shut and locked the door. "Okay, I get the picture. At five, you are certainly old enough to know your own mind." She checked his water and food dishes to ensure they were full. As if having not appreciated her insinuations, Snickerdoodle merely sniffed and turned his nose up at the food. "A man of discerning tastes as well today. Well, well."

"A cup of tea for me." Vivian turned the kettle on. "Then back to the next submission." She was thoroughly cooled down now from that last story and in need of a good distraction from her present train of thoughts.

She didn't love Mark. She knew that now. Realizing she didn't love him was harder than the break up. Yes, she had feelings for him, enough to considering spending her life with him. But she didn't *love* him? To her, love would include a burning need. Love would involve a deeper passion where the music of his soul would find an answering song in hers.

"I already know the answer, Snicker," she said, watching the dog follow her as she walked back to her brightly lit living room. She set her tea on the tray next to her favorite reading chair.

*I'm not faring too badly, all things considered.* Vivian pulled her wooly socks on, shook the tea bag out to lay it on the saucer, and wiggled to get comfortable in her chair.

After graduation, Vivian worked in the editorial department at a newspaper. Going as far as she could with the paper, Vivian grew bored. She thrived on literary excitement and the position had become mundane. The job became something she could do without much effort expended. It was time to move on, but she had become complacent. It wasn't until reading through the local newspaper, she spotted an intriguing advertisement seeking someone with editorial skills to be a reader. She was glad she seized the chance to respond to the ad.

Learning the ropes in this new medium was a competitive curve Vivian relished. The challenge was intriguing. Within the first year, she launched two very credible romance authors. In the last five years, she had added to her roster while her original two continued to flourish. These achievements added substantially to her pay cheque, allowing her to invest a little more into her tourist shop. Every time one of *her* authors wrote a new novel, their manuscripts came to her for first reading where Vivian's notes went back to the author for revision before moving up the ladder to the main editorial department. Vivian hoped to eventually make it to the editorial staff, and she was sure that day would come if she kept recommending great stories to the publishing house.

"When was the last time I took at chance?" Vivian

stirred cream in her English Breakfast tea. "Buying this place was a chance. An investment. Certainly opening the Brick 'n Brack Shop and Café with Marcy had been a chance."

The launch of her first two authors gave her the financial stability to *take the chance* as it were. Investing in the business and having Marcy as a partner gave Vivian the opportunity to build a nest egg for the future.

"Then there's the mundane. The ho-hum, no one ever writes about with any real enthusiasm. The insurance, the mortgage, the accounting, legal, and mountains of paperwork are no fun." She picked up another manuscript, taking a sip of her now slightly cooled tea.

Thinking of insurance brought her family to mind, her father the accountant and her two professional brothers. One brother was the life insurance agent she purchased her policies from. They all lived not far away and kept in touch, but weren't on top of one another. Her family thought her hobby of treasure hunting as a bit of a blight on the family. Vivian loved when the long weekend of May approached so she could start garage sailing. All summer, Thursday and Friday evenings were spent browsing for her treasures to refinish and sell in her shop. She learned a lot about tinkering and mechanics of small appliances in her hobby. She loved bringing something back to life.

"I'm like the cat lady no one admits to be to being related to. I can just hear my mother telling her society friends in her high pitched, nasal tones that her daughter has a job that pays, but…and here would be my mother's near whisper…my daughter likes those garage sales thingies. You know where people sell their own junk. It's as bad as eating left-overs. Imagine! Her father and I do all we can, but what can you do?" The *what can you do* would have to be repeated to emphasis the importance of the parental role in her life. Vivian ruffled Snickerdoodle's head. "Bla, bla, bla, is what I say to that."

Snickerdoodle, who was sitting stoutly beside her chair, seemed to be hanging on to every word she said, staring up at her with big chocolate brown eyes. Vivian was not the brooding type. She moved forward and planned. She did not regret or regress. And with that motivated thought, she smiled and went back to work.

\*\*\*\*

"We should go to a psychic!" Marcy's smile beamed with enthusiasm as they enjoyed a light lunch at Marcy's house while the kids napped.

"What? A psychic? Why?"

"Oh, it would be fun. I listened to a documentary about psychics on the radio the other week, and I've been thinking about going ever since. Have you ever been?"

"No, never." Vivian smiled. She was intrigued, but nervous to learn more. "What if they tell us something we don't want to hear?"

"I'd just tell them, no bad news." Marcy laughed and reached out to tap Vivian's arm, her kind eyes encouraging. "Come on, we'll have fun."

"Okay, I'm game," Vivian said, fork poised before her lips, feeling a slow smile rise. Excited at the prospect of an adventure, she noticed how Marcy's eyes dancing with wonder and curiosity. "Should we make it a girl's night and invite Jess and Steph?"

Marcy's brown, bobbed hair bounced on her shoulders as she picked up the phone. "Oh, yeah, that would great."

Vivian Googled local psychics on her iPhone. "Marcy, have you seen how many psychics are listed. How will we choose the right one?"

****

Vivian and her friends chose the Russian Tea House where they could combine a nice lunch along with the thrill of getting their fortunes read.

Stephanie paused, poised to open the restaurant door. She turned to face her friends, a determined look on her face as she stopped them from entering the restaurant. "No one says anything at lunch. I heard they have microphones everywhere to pick up on what you say so they seem authentic. Not a word." She mimed zippering her slips shut, locked the dead bolt, and threw away the key.

"Not hard to tell who has kids in the gang." Vivian laughed, miming the A-okay, thumbs up.

Just being the fly in the ointment, as usual, the legal council that was Jessica's personality stripe piped up. "But they could be listening right now," she whispered.

Vivian waved her hand at her giggling friends to enter the Tea House.

They decided beforehand that after their lunch and the readings, they would head to Marcy's house to review their fortunes. Marcy, the planner of the bunch, had scheduled the whole day and discussed her reading first.

"Well, the fortune teller as much as called me a control freak." Marcy laughed, her face contorted in a farce of mock anger. "George will be so pleased to hear that."

Jess, clad in fit-to-suit silk, dusty pink blouse, paired with beige slacks, crossed her slender legs in the over-sized chair. "Big surprise there," she said. "Don't waste time on what we already know, tell us something we don't know."

"Well, I opted for the tea leaves and tarot cards. I never imagined I would get to choose two forms of reading. I thought they would just do their thing." Marcy reached for her tea and sipped before continuing. "She said George and I were well matched and would live a long life together."

Stephanie, a whip-smart firecracker of the realty world, was never one to waste time or words. "Sigh," she said, settling her petite form more comfortably on the coach. "Get on with it."

Vivian's friends continued.

Marcy said there was a baby girl in her future, Jessica said her law practice would be a success, and Stephanie confirmed she had celiac disease, which explained why she was ill after most meals.

While Vivian's friends hotly debated the accuracy of their readings, she reflected on not knowing what to expect from her fortune, or if she expected anything, but she was surprised at Madame Rose's attire. Vivian assumed the psychic would be a Gypsy-looking woman with at least a crystal ball nearby, but Madame Rose resembled a modern day woman, wearing a black pencil skirt and white blouse.

The only information Vivian had relayed to the woman was her name and date of birth at the beginning of the conversation. She contemplated the psychic's advice, recounting Madame Rose's words. "Your number is a five with an undercurrent of four. You love the drama." Her voice was hauntingly husky as though coming from the deepest reaches of Vivian's own soul. "You want…no, crave adventure, but the four keeps you to home. You're loyal, fiercely passionate, yet you are holding back. You must feel that craving deeply on the inside. That craving of adventure is here in your cards over and over. You want to be spontaneous yet you restrain. Why are you holding back? What are you waiting for? You have so much to give." Madame Rose paused and nudged the glasses on her nose with her forefinger. "I'm not telling you anything you don't already know, am I?"

The polished woman stared at Vivian with a question in her magnified eyes, but didn't offer to discuss the question. She simply took Vivian's hand, and then read her palm. Brushing her fingers lightly over Vivian's right palm, the psychic smiled. "You will find what you seek. *It* is out there. The answer to the question you ask is, *yes*. Do you know what that means?"

Vivian nodded. "I think so, yes."

"Be honest with yourself, and know it's okay to seek your heart's desire. Do you know what *it* is?"

"Yes." Vivian nodded again. She was completely mesmerized by the psychic sitting across the table. Madame Rose's voice had a slight horse tenor of an active, indulgent smoker. She was a woman obvious use to commanding attention, and the theatrical delivery of her *reading* had Vivian riveted to every word. It was as though the psychic was in Vivian's head reading her innermost reflections. Contemplations Vivian seldom even admitted to herself.

Madame Rose continued. "Money is not your motivator and for that reason you will always have money. Adventure is the key to your success. You want it, you crave it, and it's right out there waiting for you. Stop trying to be someone you are not."

Vivian grew scared of the brash lady with the hypnotic black eyes—the only psychic-like feature she owned.

Squeezing Vivian's hand, Madame Rose stared deep into Vivian's soul. "If you do not set your heart free, you will wither and die unhappy, and unfulfilled."

"What a cow!" said Jess after Vivian relayed her fortune to her friends.

"No way," said Steph. "I didn't believe a word the turban wearer told me. I thought I got the dud."

"No." Marcy shook her head. "No, that will not happen. Don't give that crazy psychic's words any consideration. What a crock! Look at you! While we change diapers and attend house chores, you're free to do whatever you want. That woman definitely read you wrong!"

Chapter Two

As weeks went by and winter thawed to spring, the psychic's words danced like a mantra in Vivian's head. Yes, a passionate love was possible. And yes, romance was worth searching—worth waiting for.

"I think a vacation is what you need. How long has it been since you went somewhere nice?" Marcy turned to Vivian as they walked to the park with her children.

"Well, Mark and I went to…"

"In that case, too long, eh?" Marcy interrupted.

"Too long," Vivian agreed, cuddling Isaac, while Marcy's oldest son, Jon, bolted like a shot toward the slide.

Who would Vivian go away with? She had never gone on vacation alone. It's not that she was afraid to travel alone. She just never contemplated going off by herself before. She did lots of things by herself obviously, she was a single woman. Being alone in your own back yard was distinctly different then being single while travelling. Women did it all the time, but could she? The prospect of travelling somewhere foreign just seemed lonely and, to be honest, a little needy, like she would be seeking something. But maybe she was?

She still smarted from the last time she attended one of her mother's society balls by herself. Vivian hadn't imagined the stares and the whispered words behind pale manicured hands. Her mother's upper class friends had treated Vivian as though she was diseased, or in mourning. They talked a little louder, leaning toward her with their head slightly bent in sympathy. She despised their watchful eyes looking upon her with pity at being alone.

\*\*\*\*

*Mackenzie Blackwell stood at the helm of his full rigged ship, the Navigator, squinting at the setting sun. His large, black Labrador Retriever sat stoically at his side, also appearing to watch the horizon for land. Tiller, the watchman in the masthead, said he spotted land to the west.*

*From his current position, Mackenzie could not see any sign of land, which they hoped to reach by nightfall. But if he had timed everything correctly, Tiller, the monkey-like youngster should be correct, as they had been pushing for Halifax harbour for the last week to off load their cargo of rum and other contraband.*

*Mackenzie's strong tanned features gave him every air of authority. He checked the sky and the tack of the wind. Reaching a slender fingered hand into the breast pocket of his oilskin, he retrieved his scope to get a better look at the horizon. The fingers grasping the instrument looked more suitable for playing the piano than running a ship. But that was another life. As his narrow wrist snapped the spyglass to its full extension, he commanded the master, the man trusted to know all the routes and the weather, better known as the ships keeper, to maintain the current course.*

*"Aye, aye, capt'n," Burke responded.*

*Though no one would know by looking at him, his face a careful mask, Mackenzie always grew antsy as he approached land. Land was dangerous. Land meant patrols and possible conflict. In the open sea, he could best and outrun just about any ship of the line. But being close to land changed the odds. A careful gambler, Mackenzie didn't favour when the odds were not on his side. The only time he chose to port was when he was in need of supplies and ready to make his drop, which meant his ship was weighted down with cargo and not as swift. This in turn meant there was always the chance that more than one frigate, be it English or French could corner, leaving no room to manoeuvre and escape.*

Ohhh, this was just the kind of book Vivian loved to sink her teeth into. *I could get into the romance of this guy. The whole historical adventure of sailing away on the high seas. I can almost reach out and run my fingers through his too long hair, taste the salt of the sea on his lips.* Her tongue poked out to moisten her lips.

Reading the first three chapters easily, Vivian typed her report of recommendation for this submission to the publisher. Sending an email to the author, requesting the next three chapters for preview, was a delight in Vivian's day. The author was an unknown, but if the story kept the momentum going, Vivian was sure they would have a winner. But she was getting ahead of the game. She would have to wait and see what the next chapters brought.

As she sat at her computer composing the submission report, she had an urge so strong she acted on the impulse before she could second-guess what she was doing. She typed *learn to sail* in the search prompt. She wanted the adventure she always read about. Now was the time.

*What am I doing? I can't just fly off somewhere to learn how to sail. Especially alone. Mother would have a hay day, saying my actions were foolish. Maybe if I were still a kid—still in my twenties. Maybe, hmmm, but I'm going anyway.*

She looked at the manuscript. A piece of the sea, the adventure of being in the open ocean, and a sexy man at the helm. This was the theme she loved in every romance. *A theme that would make for an exciting and unusual vacation.* Vivian grew more excited with the idea.

Before she could think too much about a sailing cruise where she would learn how to sail, she went on Expedia booking her flights, hotel, and the boat charter.

"You did what?" Vivian's mother screeched in a most unladylike fashion during their family dinner. It was Sunday and her mother had just placed the turkey on the table. Her mother didn't cook often, but when she did, the meal consisted of one of three dishes— turkey, pot roast, or ham.

"What are you going on about?" Vivian's father, Peter, chimed in with his resolute, accountant's voice. He placed a turkey leg to the side of his plate. "Didn't you learn anything with Mark? Get your head out of the clouds. My gawd learning to sail, that's crazy!"

"Your father's right. It's simply not proper for a woman to go off alone. You don't know what the crew members will be like. In fact, it's complete foolishness. Cancel the trip."

Vivian explained how much she anticipated learning something new. "Geez, can't you see what a great opportunity this is for me. I don't want to be that person that grows old watching other people live their exciting lives on TV. I want to be the person having fun." Vivian cut into her meat, stuffing a chunk in her mouth without tasting it. "As for the crew members, they're a lovely maritime family who have built ships for generations. They now take tourists out and teach them the ancient art of sailing."

"Listen to you. What romantic rubbish," Peter said in an all-knowing smug way, determined that he knew all and no one could tell him different. He mixed the turkey gravy with his mash potatoes, picking up a scoop-full of the creamy vegetable on his fork. He was poised, ready to place the blend in his mouth when he paused. Waving the heaping fork in gesture, his lips parted in a slight sneer. "You sound like you wrote the ad for them."

Vivian loved her family. She had to. Loving her family was a pre-requisite. *No matter what, you have to love your family. Do other children feel like me? Like they were plucked from a stork, because I can't imagine how I came from my parent's loins. I'm different. Too different. They know and I know, but still try to change me. Why must everything be an argument? Some grand debate?*

"You've both made up your mind about this trip without actually listening to a word I say." Vivian lowered her fork to the side of the china plate, finished with arguing with them and resolute in her decision to proceed whether her parents supported her choice or not.

"We're listening," her mother said with an exaggerated strain in her nasal tones. She dabbed her over-lined lips with her snow-white napkin. Lowering the large cotton square back to her lap, and taking the time to fold the linen just right over her perfectly creased pants, she finally raised her green-melon coloured eyes to Vivian. The image of motherly concern etched her porcelain cheeks. "Rebecca's daughter, Nancy, just got married. You remember her from summer camp?" When Vivian stared at her mother un-answering, her mother continued. "Rebecca thought for sure marriage was never going to happen for Nancy. Wild that one." She paused and rolled her eyes, before focusing her attention back to Vivian. "Anyway, Rebecca encouraged her daughter to go on one of those on-line dating sites and now she's married. No more foolishness."

It was the same old story. Always a different example, but every conversation ended with a statement about how Vivian wasn't married. Headline news in this house in bold capital letters—Vivian Margaret was not married.

Starring at her mother biting her lip with her front teeth, Vivian fought the urge to throw her napkin on the table and leave.

Agghh, Vivian wanted to scream, but her parents would see it as an emotional collapse and recommend a *nice* doctor, who wasn't married. Why did they only focus on her failures? Why couldn't they see her success—the café and shop? Oh, yes, they'd say that accomplishment was due to her business partner's vast abilities as a chef. What about her fairly prominent position within a publishing house doing a job she loved? No, not tangible either. Reality remained, Vivian wasn't married and hadn't provided them with grandkids. Her brothers married and reproduced soon after. Obviously her parents thought something was wrong with her, and as a result, they treated her like a child.

Vivian tried again to justify her plans, taking a different tract outlining her trip as a simple vacation. "It's just a chance to get away. I need a break."

"Hell of a time to take a break," her father jumped in, having finished his dinner and wiping his face with his napkin, "Leaving your business partner, with two small kids of her own, to hold down the fort." He shook his head. "Running off is irresponsible, that's what I would call this little *break* of yours. We should review your first quarter financial statement before you go running off somewhere. Maybe it's time for a reality break. Time to get your priories in order." He emphasised his words, lifting his hand to make air quotes.

Vivian pressed her lips together and didn't speak of her trip during the remainder of dinner. She allowed her brothers and their wives to monopolize the conversation, finally releasing a sigh of relief when it was time to leave.

As she gathered her coat and purse from the closet, Vivian's mother held her purse while she pulled her coat over her arms. "Now, promise me." Her mother tapped Vivian's cheek. "You'll cancel this foolish trip and plan something nice with one of your girl friends."

Having endured the battle of dinner, Vivian would not surrender. Taking a step back from her mother's reach, she straightened her shoulders. "No, Mother. I'm not going to promise. You think I'm foolish, but I'm a thirty-one year old woman who will do as I please." She grabbed her purse from her mother's hands.

Her mother rolled her eyes and storm off to the kitchen.

"Now who's acting like a child," Vivian muttered under her breath as her brother walked toward her.

"Don't fuss, Sis," Tyler said, reaching in the closet to get his wife's jacket. "You know our folks are the way they are. So set in their ways. Mother wouldn't think of getting groceries at a different store for heaven's sake. You go for it. Have fun. You deserve it. I'll even drive you to the airport." He gave her a kiss on the cheek.

Vivian turned to leave, smiling for the first time all evening.

Chapter Three

"Shit," Tuck muttered, slapping the palm of his hand flat on the water's surface. Taking a deep breath, he lifted the goggles from his eyes and settled them on the top of his head.

"Brother, you just don't know how sweet this is." Nate gloated as he boosted out of the water with one arm to perch on the side of the pool. "Kicking my little brother's ass in the pool, at long last!"

"Yeah, yeah, little brother, whatever. You're older by what, eight minutes?" Tuck grinned, moving into Nate's lane to smile at his twin. Though Nate's features were similar to his own, they were not identical. "Enjoy victory while you can."

As Tuck alighted from the pool, Nate continued the banter. "What you need, little brother..." He wrapped his arm around Tuck's shoulders as they headed to the men's dressing room. "Is a good woman. Enough of the fast food crap. You need a good woman to keep you home, happy, and satisfied."

"We all can't be as lucky as you to grab them out of the cradle and convince them you are the only one in the world. No, some of us have to hunt." Tuck smiled, happy his brother and Emily, high school sweethearts that they were, had each other. They gave Tuck hope that perhaps someday, when he was ready, he would settle down. But the trauma, or drama, depending on how you looked at it, of the last couple of years, made him shy of opening up to anyone again. Burned is what some may call him, and twice shy.

Nate walked to the men's shower humming *We Are the Champions* anthem while Tuck hung his goggles in his locker and grabbed a towel to wrap around his waist. Tuck and his brother were reservists in the Coast Guard. Tuck having just recently re-joined upon his untimely return home, while Nate, who never left home, made Tuck's reintegration that much smoother. Rescue reservists were expected to be available in states of emergency and obligated to maintain a certain level of fitness.

"I have to get my time up if I'm going to be any good in the open ocean." Tuck, a rescue swimmer, bemoaned his time in the pool today, while Nate was a marine ships navigator and didn't need to be fast. "Just goes to show, swimming's not enough. The last couple of years away from the fight of the open ocean have certainly taken its toll, if you can beat me."

"Don't let losing to me get you down, little brother. You can always try again next week." Nate flashed a smug smile as his large hands soaped his heavily muscled chest. Years of pulling ropes and the heavy ships labour had made his body as hard as a ship's deck.

"I hear there's a single this trip." Nate changed the subject as Tuck stepped in the shower beside his brother. While Nate was wide across the shoulders and powerfully built, Tuck was lean muscle, which made him look taller, even though they were exactly the same height. "Ma and Emily got into quite the conversation when Ma said it's not right for a woman to be travellin' alone. She's so old fashioned. Emily had been fired up about her talk with Ma last night at supper. I reminded Emily, she's known Ma long enough to know when she should drop the subject."

"I'm sure that won you points with the wife," Tuck said, casting his brother what he knew was a knowing look. "Your Emily's a firecracker though. She can't drop anything." His words garbled as he tilted his face directly into the shower spray, loving the feel of the water sluicing across his body. If he had found an Emily, he'd never let her go. Passion and compassion combined in equal measures. She always sought out the underdog. "She'll give Ma a go as Matriarch of this clan before long."

"Emily thinks it's grand this woman wants to learn to sail. I have to agree it's brave, if nothing else. In all the year's we've been running the Learn to Sail School, this is the first time a woman has come on her own."

"Maybe she misunderstood and thought it was a *sale* school for shopping." Tuck guffawed at his own wit. "I'll have to spell check the website."

"Ohmigod, imagine the shock if that were the case." Nate joined Tuck's laughter.

Tuck's family have been a sea faring family for generations. They had their fortunes attached to the ocean tides in one manner or another. Just like the ocean moulds and shapes the environment upon which it abuts, so too had his family adapted over the generations. From merchant sailors, sometimes referred to as pirating, depending on who was telling the story and whether they were in their cups or not, to fleet runners, fishermen, and ship builders, to modern day teachers of the ancient technique of sailing, the

MacLean's continued to align themselves with the briny deep.

Tuck found his feet enveloped in the bosom of his family's welcoming embrace after being away for many years, striving to find his own foothold in the world. Sometimes, when he considered what was and what may have been, the reality had been a devastating awakening to realize his feet were better suited to the place he longed to escape for so many years. This had been home all along, where comfort found him.

"So a woman on her own. I hadn't thought much about the booking when it came in." Tuck ran a towel over his body, and then glanced over his shoulder at his brother. "Billy's off tomorrow, so Ma's sending me to pick up our guest at the airport. I have to run to the city to get some stuff anyway so it's no big deal. We need an ADSL as a back up to the Wi-Fi and the CCD needs to be replaced."

"Oh, little brother, how you turn me on when you start talking dirty. Those FMG's mixed with the OMG's of cyber space." Nate glanced under his raised arm, smirking at Tuck. He rinsed the shampoo from his hair, shaking his head like a dog, splattering Tuck. Nick uproariously laughed. "Here I am telling you about an eligible woman coming to our fair town and you respond with geek talk."

Tuck didn't have time for women. Not seriously at any rate. When he divorced Suzy, after less than a year of marriage, the last thing he wanted to consider was entering into a relationship. Sure, the divorce had been finalized for more than year, but it had made him gun-shy at the very thought of commitment. Casual, to cover his needs, is where he lived. It's where he intended to stay.

"If you only knew, old man, how truly sexy the geek talk can get in certain circles, you'd actually pay attention when someone's trying to teach you something." Tuck flicked his towel at his brother before wiping the splatter drops from Nate's dog-style spray across his face. "You'd learn how to check your own email and stop bugging me every time you want to order something online."

Nate ducked and ran to his locker, dodging the sting of Tuck's towel.

A recurrent of sadness swept Tuck. If only his brother knew. At one time, Tuck did have it all. A successful business, the high-rise penthouse condo, the trophy wife. Oh, she was a sweet bit. Reliable too, so long as Tuck had money. He should have known better. Everyone warned him about Suzy. And goddamnit, they were right. As soon as things got tough, his wife left. The condo was next and finally, despite his best efforts, his business.

Tuck ran his fingers through his damp hair, refusing to give in to the past. Recently Emily and Nate seemed intent on matchmaking, pointing out one local girl or another as eligible. Tuck would have nothing more to do with romance. He was done with love. It was as gone as his wife, his business, and the life he had built in the city.

****

Vivian had been nervous, despite her outward bravado with her friends. Although she had previously spoken to Mrs. MacLean, who insisted Vivian call her Lynette, her stomach still twisted in knots when her brother drove her to the airport.

"Enjoy yourself," Tyler said, carrying her two bags to the terminal. "We've got Snicker. You know the kids love him and may not give him back." He laughed, and placed a hand on her shoulder. "Really, you can count on us to take good care of him."

She hugged him and kissed his cheek, before checking in.

Lynette MacLean had said they lived in a small town a couple of hours from the airport. She reassured Vivian *one of the boys* would pick her up and drive her to the local bed and breakfast, cosily called, The Mariner's Roost. Vivian would stay at the Inn the first half of her two-week vacation, while she learned the basics of the ship prior to launch. Thereafter she would be at sea for five nights. After the trip, she planned to stay a couple extra days to take in the sights before returning home.

She had high hopes for her adventure, but missed home already. Her cozy cottage and the shop where she loved to get dirty playing with her gadgets and treasures, restoring them to their original condition. Then she'd display her wares in the gift corner of the café to sell to someone else who would appreciated the hidden treasures in life. She missed home, where potted lovelies grew on her back patio, and where her garden and rose bush grew in one spot surrounded by weeds— the trouble spot by the garage where nothing but weeds would root despite her best efforts. She missed home, where Snickerdoodle ran free amongst the acres of farm land, never caged, and slept at her feet by the fire.

Vivian had wisely booked her trip before the start of the tourist season for a number of reasons, not least of which it being cheaper. This time of year meant her business was less busy and most important, easier for her to leave her work and obligations for a while. She knew Marcy would keep the shop in fine stead however, Vivian remembered her father's words that left her with an added pang of regret thinking he was right and she had left her best friend in a lurch.

\*\*\*\*

The little boy, sitting beside her on the plane, dug his finger into his nose surely sinking the digit through to the knuckle. His mother, reading a book in the aisle seat, was oblivious to her son's quest for gold. To hide her smile, Vivian turned to the window to watch the land fall to the ocean. Somehow a little boy picking his nose seemed natural, almost cute.

Speaking of natural, she wondered if she was too old to be going away alone on some quest for—what exactly she didn't know? The slight turbulence broke her reverie as the plane turned and banked toward the land for arrival. She watched the green hills and roadways come into focus. A fissure of excitement skipped through her veins as she realized she was really going through with this trip. Leaving on her own for a couple of weeks seemed so completely unlike her. Nervousness and anticipation overwhelmed her, wondering what would happen over the next few days.

The plane shuttered on an air pocket during the descent and she grabbed the hand rests. The little boy beside her laid his small hands on top of her own. Vivian was comforted by his gentle touch. She smiled down to the round face with big brown eyes.

"It's okay," he said, patting her hand. "It'll be okay."

Vivian nodded, placing her right hand over his.

"Thank you. You've made me feel better." She smiled, and sat straight to regain her poise. The little boy smiled, revealing the loss of his bottom teeth. His mother spared him a quick glance before returning to her book.

Vivian released her grip on the armrest by window, and gazed at the approaching tarmac. About to begin her adventure, her stomach curled with apprehension. Her quest for fun teased that little fissure of something inside her she had always tried to squash when it peaked the surface. She inhaled a deep breath and smiled, awaiting the first step in her journey.

****

"Well dear, this is not an auspicious start to your vacation," Lynette lamented when Vivian called her from the airport arrival area to report no one was here to retrieve her. Vivian didn't expect such a volume of embarrassment and frustration in the older woman's voice. She wouldn't want to get on Lynette's bad side and knew the driver would suffer the brunt of older lady's wrath. "Where can that boy be? I'll skin him alive when he returns. What's your cell number, dear? I'll contact him and call you right back."

Vivian pulled her cell out of her purse and scrunched her face. One bar. No cell service.

"I'm afraid my cell number won't do much good. The signal's pretty weak inside the airport."

"Well, if I don't call you back in five minutes, you call me back from the payphone land line and reverse the charges."

Vivian agreed and waited. When her cell did not ring, she decided to move forward on her own. *Taking that first step is part of the adventure.* Where was the fun, if she couldn't take charge of her own destiny?

With a sense of confidence, she smiled, walked to the payphone, and called Mrs. MacLean to relay her decision.

"I can't reach his cell phone either! Honest to God! Excuse my language, but I will brain that boy of mine! You won't believe this, but this is not usual. The Parson's and the Jordan's were picked up just yesterday, no issues at all. I am so sorry, dear."

Vivian didn't understand what *braining* her son meant, but it certainly didn't sound good. "Don't fuss, Mrs. MacL...Lynette. I'll get a car and a map, and will see you tomorrow. I'll be fine, really. Don't fuss."

"I'm an old woman dear, fussin' is what I do. It makes me happy," she said.

Vivian had a mental image of a hen-like woman sitting on her eggs waiting for them to hatch.

Lynette sighed. "Okay dear. You come by tomorrow for lunch and we'll chat. It'll give us an opportunity to get to know one another before Randy and Nate, that's my dear husband and *other* son, train you on the boat basics with the rest."

Vivian could get accustomed to being called *dear*. She understood the word to be part of the vernacular of the area, but her own mother had never used the flattering remark. The endearment was so charming Vivian couldn't wait to meet Lynette, but pitied Lynette's son, whom Vivian assumed to be about seventeen to eighteen-years old, learning the ropes and utterly failing in the one task given to him today. She wouldn't want to be him when he returned home for supper today.

She bent to place the information package into her

carry all, and reaching for the long handle of her suitcase, she stepped away from the payphone. At the same time she was being swept away with a renewed sense of self-assurance, Vivian suddenly collided with a solid object—the hard wall being the chest to a very tall man. Her gaze travelled the distance from his brown loafers, to his casual beige khakis, and untucked cotton shirt with rolled cuffs to the elbows. Continuing her scrutiny, she eyed the open collar revealing a tanned neck, and then a beautiful smile. Her gaze moved to his formed forearms that lengthened to strong hands, which she quickly realized were holding her shoulders in a steady hold.

At five-foot eleven, Vivian made eye contact with most men and not familiar to looking up. In heels, which she loved to wear when the opportunity struck, she would be taller than most. Her height had been a major source of self-consciousness when she was younger, but she now relished it, loving the authority it provided her with.

Tearing her glance from the hands on her shoulders to his ruddy cheeks, strong jaw line, and well formed lips, she made her way back a set of eyes that resembled the wind-whipped sea. She had never stared into such gorgeous silver-grey eyes, Vivian teetered on her stilettos. "Oh, I'm so sorry."

"You okay?" he said, his lips very close to her face. Amusement and appreciation were evident in his gaze as it travelled over her face. Uninvited, his hands remained on her shoulders, sending warm currents down her spine as he continued to study her.

Vivian moved her lips to speak, but was lost in his cocked half-grin and mesmerizing eyes. The momentary spell was broken when he said, "Hey, you're tall for a woman."

Cold water dosed the sudden warmth enjoyed by his hands splayed across her narrow shoulders. "Like I've never heard that before." She didn't bother to hide the ice in her tone. His simple words had thrown thrown her back to her awkward high school days when she wanted the boys to notice her and not her towering height.

With her balance restored, she shrugged his hands from her shoulders and turned on her heel to walk away. Her long legs ate up the distance as she made her way toward the car rental wicket, bemoaning the waste of such a good looking guy. "Maybe I should have asked him, how's the air up there for you?"

No matter how old she got, a negative twist on her height always smarted. She had constantly suffered from people making fun—asking if she played basketball or how the air was up there.

It seemed okay for a guy to be tall—as if expected and to be achieved. But a tall girl? No, a girl had to be petite, small, and doll-like, like her friend Stephanie. Most woman couldn't attain Stephanie's perfection, but ironically, it had been Stephanie who brought her up short, pardon the pun, when Vivian had been a teenager about to start University, but still trying to hide her height by slouching her shoulders and bending her knees unnecessarily lower when she walked, trying to be invisible.

Stephanie had grabbed Vivian's arm roughly, stopping her in her tracks. Stephanie explained how she hated wearing heels just to be seen—to be noticed, and if she was as tall as Vivian, she'd glory in it. She ordered Vivian to flaunt her height, to show what God gave her and never, ever, be ashamed.

It was weird how one person's words could bring about such a change, but from that day on, Vivian walked straighter—held her head taller, facing life head on. She wore heels when she wanted, and any man who was intimidated by her height weren't worth a second look. She quickly learned that as soon as she forgot about her own insecurity, so did most men.

But there were always exceptions.

As she continued to the car rental wicket, she could still feel the warmth of those strong fingers on her shoulders. Vivian's thoughts wandered, imagining the magic those hands could invoke, if invited, to the rest of her body. A shiver chased down her spine.

Chapter Four

Tuck welcomed the distraction of staring at the lovely lady as much as he dreaded the phone call he had to make to his mother. Watching the retreating figure, his appreciation of the view turned to a chuckle at her murmured comment about *the air up there*, which he had heard a zillion times. The momentary diversion of a beautiful woman was just what he needed before tackling his mother. Taking one last glance at that spiky black hair and those lovely long legs, ending in red she-devil stilettos, brought a touch of perspiration to his upper lip, which he quickly wiped away with his forefinger. "Too bad, she's not the woman I'm looking for."

Tuck shook his head, returning his attention to his reason for standing by the bank of payphones. "Goddamnit, where the heck is Margaret?" He reached into his pockets for change as he moved toward the phone the woman had just vacated, smelling the faint scent of coconuts as he lifted the receiver.

Not being able to get a damn cell signal in the airport was the icing on the proverbial cake. He had been here an hour already. He even waited for the last person to trickle off the flight Margaret was suppose to be on.

He checked with the flight staff. "No," the grey-haired woman confirmed. "Everyone has departed the plane and we're preparing for the next batch of passengers. Perhaps you missed your friend walking by. Did you try luggage?"

Tuck jogged to baggage claim holding his *Margaret* sign like some limo driver waiting for the rock star to arrive. This was typically his younger cousin's job, but Billy had final exams today and struggling to get his marks up so he could get accepted into film school. So *pickup* was Tuck's job. *Lucky me.*

All the women he thought looked like a Margaret walked by without any interest in him even when he waggled the sign in front of them like some sort of vagabond begging for spare change.

"Margaret? What in the name of all that is holy are you talking about, boy? The woman's name is Vivian!" The exasperation in his mother's voice was more than obvious. "Vivian!"

*Vivian.* Tuck rolled the name in his mind as his mother continued to berate him. He learned early on how to tune-out while she vented. *Vivian,* now there was a name to conjure an image. Margaret, on the other hand, brought to his mind an old auntie of ninety-five telling stories to the kids when she visited, smacking her lips together to hold her dentures in place.

"Ma." Tuck tried to get a word in. "Ma, please. Cool down and listen to me. The plaque card says Margaret. I'm not the one who writes the plaque cards. I'm just the errand boy you sent to pick her up."

"What? Your dad does those and we've never had a mistake...until now."

Tuck rolled his eyes at his mother's jab—a reminder he was the newest member to the family business. "Yeah, I know, Ma." Tuck sighed.

"Ya know I didn't mean that in a bad way toward you."

He knew his mother's sails were deflated with the knowledge she could no longer blame him for the mishap. As the self-appointed matriarch of the family, she liked having everyone home, and his leaving still smarted an angry sore that never healed.

Tuck had been a computer programmer, a good one, until eighteen-months ago. He loved the art of programming, the digging down layer after layer of computer labyrinths until he got exactly what he wanted from the machine. He was a creator and worked in the city for some big-named companies before turning to consulting, and adding clients of his own.

He'd still be doing his dream job now if it hadn't been for a self-serving accountant, a rather creative accountant who should be jailed. Add in a glitter and glam girl friend with the spending habits of a French prostitute and whamo! Game over. Damn tech bubble. When that thing went bust, everything Tuck had strived for his whole life burst with it.

Marching out of the airport toward his parked car, Tuck's mood grew dark. His easy smile of only minutes before evaporated and replaced with frown lines creasing his brow.

The MacLean family had been brought up on the water. They learned to sail young, built and repaired boats, but Tuck had wanted more. What that was now, he couldn't quite recall. All he remembered was having the burn to put small town life behind him. He wanted to experience life beyond the rugged coastlines of Nova Scotia's South Shore. Wanted to be away from the place where everybody knew your business, or where everybody *thought* they knew your business. He wanted to be more than a MacLean, known for ship building.

After University, paid for by his stint in the Coast Guard as a rescue swimmer, Tuck left the craggy harbour and set out as an intern. He quickly moved up the corporate ladder in pursuit of...what? What had been so clear to him then was now a fog.

Tuck had been something all right. For a while at least. There were parties, dinners, and lots of glitter. Oh, the accolades. He couldn't get enough of those. Ego, ego, ego. How could he have even considered what was important?

What a fool he had been. The girl, the clients, his house, and his business, in that order, all gone. Amazing enough, his girl had disappeared faster than the slimy accountant or his business partner.

Tuck raised a hand to his forehead, feeling the lines of bitterness running across his brow. He should have listened to his mother, but didn't dare tell her that. She had told him to always listen to his gut—to listen to the warning signal that goes off in your head when you first meet someone. But he chose not to listen to his mother or his gut. He got swept away in the glamour of the moment, and then fell hard, going through not one, but three divorces at once. The partnership agreement, the winding down corporately of his business, and with his wife.

He didn't even speak his former wife's name in his parent's house. His mother would purse her lips and walk away whenever the subject of Tuck's life in the city came up in conversation. She never mention Suzy's name. His ma made no bones about ever caring about his marriage to Suzy or anything that occurred while he was away. Thankfully, he had a fall-back plan. The safety net many didn't have—a family that cared.

Despite their affection and open-arms welcome, coming home had been humiliating. He lived with Nate, Emily, and the kids for a while until he found his feet again. Family being family, they cushioned him, providing the much need balm for his aching soul. Helping him recover.

When his dad offered him a job in the family business, he was not too proud to say yes, grateful for the opportunity. His mom, dad, and even Nate all had some great ideas on where they wanted to take the business, but no way of execution. Once he listened to their strategy, he knew he could take their ideas and make them a reality on social media and the internet. Through his marketing genius, Tuck was able to redesign and develop a plan to bring attention to the business.

At least to his family, he was still their Tuck, and he thanked God for that. For as high as he thought he had climbed and the length of time it had taken to get there, the fall was fast, furious, and without mercy.

His family, who were his one true constant, didn't seem to care one way or another about his past mistakes, as long as he came home. They loved him as they always did. They never made him feel like the failure he thought he was. Being needed made all the difference.

With Tuck taking the joint roles of IT and Marketing, the family business had swelled, going from breakeven two years ago, to this year's seasonal projects doubling their profit. With a little web access customers were booking on-line. Tuck had linked their

Learn to Sail website to major resort and tourism databases making it easy for people to find them. Once they found us, Ma reeled them in with her earthy charm and straight forward ways.

"People are attracted to clear speaking and good common sense," his mother told him as she reeled in another booking—her third that week. "Who'da thought that manners would be so rare this day in age."

Tuck resumed tuning into his mother on the other end of the phone, grateful for the break of his reverie. "I swear your dad is losing his marbles, one at a time, of course. Vivian Margaret is the lady's full name. Never mind now, though. You probably walked right past her. She's finding her own way. Just come on home, sweetie, and drive carefully. Your ole ma loves ya, ya know."

"I know, Ma. See you soon."

Tuck understood how the mix-up could happen. He didn't think his dad was *losing his marbles* at all. Filing a sailing manifest required the full name of all their clients, ids, and passports in preparation for voyage. The ship would be crossing international waters lines. Authorities required all necessary paperwork to be filed by the ship and crew members. His father just got the two names mixed up. Could happen to anyone. Despite understanding the error, Tuck did worry at times. His parents weren't getting any younger, regardless of their spry ways.

He shook his head, clearing his mind of the disheartening thought and headed for his car. He paused as he exited the airport to inhale a cleansing breath, and then stepped off the curb in the white-striped pedestrian crosswalk. He quickly jumped back as a rental car flew pass him, almost hitting him. His heart rate racing, Tuck peered at the car as it sped away to see the driver's bent head looking at something other than the road. Probably a map.

*Damn tourist, never paying attention to where they are going.*

****

What luck. Vivian smiled as she drove away from the airport in her rental. The car had an iPod adaptor direct to the car speakers. Another secret joy she rarely shared with anyone was her love for music. It gave her a sense of freedom she craved.

She plugged in her music and turned her attention back to the road. She quickly spun the steering wheel to prevent from veering off the road, thankful the other lane was clear of vehicles. "Whoa, that was close."

With the miss-mash of roads and too many signs leading out of the airport, she took the wrong exit. Stopping on the shoulder of the road, to use the GPS on her iPhone, she managed to get her bearings and right herself on the correct path. After a series of bypasses and overpasses, within a half hour she was enjoying the scenic shore drive. Green, green, and more green dispersed with flowering trees, vivid vegetation, and picturesque houses set atop storybook hills directly out of fairy tales, greeted her as she travelled the secondary highway.

*If I were a writer, I would surly write about this countryside.* The ocean to one side, and the fields and farms to the other. A soft breeze blowing, good music playing, and the shining sun, the perfect start to her vacation.

Finally reaching the quaint town and finding her

lodging was an easy task as there wasn't much to the small town of Macintosh. The large white house of The Mariner's Roost set upon a small hill. The driveway curved around the house with parking at the back. Stepping out of the car, she stretched and inhaled, filling her lungs with the salty air. She paused for a moment to breathe in the beautiful stretch of green-grey ocean scenery.

Vivian rummaged in the trunk and pulled out her carry-all and one piece of luggage. She was ready for a good night's sleep to recover from the long day of travel, and a fresh start tomorrow, but after marvelling in the spectacular view, Vivian decided on a quick run before grabbing a bite to eat. She laid a hand on her stomach to calm the flutter of excitement.

Checking in to her lodging cooled her curiosity. Mrs. Ethel Fraser was a plain-dressed woman who spoke frankly and without inflection.

"You really are here on your own?" Ethel resumed her seat as Vivian signed the old-fashioned register.

"Yes." Vivian glanced at the paper, shaking her head at the woman's shock of a woman travelling alone. Vivian wondered if Mrs. Fraser was a friend of her mother.

"No husband at all?"

"No, none."

"Divorced, then?"

"No, never married." Vivian glanced at the blue-haired woman with a tight bun held severely on the top of her head.

"Um hum." Ethel stood to stow the register in the drawer. "I'll show you up to your room then, will I?" She walked around the heavily polished desk, the high gloss repelling any thought that dust would dare settle.

"Yes, please."

Despite her frank questioning, Vivian liked Ethel instantly, seeing her as a friendly sort who was one of those people who needed to *fit* everyone she met.

"If you could hold my dinner until I return from a quick run, I would appreciate it." Vivian smiled.

Ethel frowned. "What are you running from?"

"I'm not running from anything." Vivian laughed. "I'm simply cramped from the long travel. I think a good stretch would be best to help me relax."

Ethel's face seemed to lack any form of expression, as if she couldn't understand someone's need to exercise.

Ethel guided Vivian to her room, unlocked the door, and shuffled back down the corridor. Vivian closed the door and glanced around the room. More spacious than it appeared from the outside, a dormer window with a cushioned seat graced one wall, while the bed, piled high with a fluffy duvet, filled the one opposite, leaving room for a bathroom and a small chest of drawers to complete the space.

Pulling out her sneakers, shorts, and T-shirt from her luggage, she quickly changed. She checked the charge on her iPhone, laced up her runners, and was stretching her legs when Ethel knocked on the door.

She handed Vivian a map. "Don't get lost, dear. My number is on the back and I've circled where you are now."

Vivian smiled. There was the use of *dear* again that warmed Vivian's heart. It made her feel special. Maybe the older woman had emotion after all and was simply incapable of showing it on her face.

Taking the map from Ethel, Vivian scanned it quickly, noting both the circle indication for the house and the number before folding it neatly in her pocket. She secured her iPhone in her arm-band. "Okay, thanks. I'll be about an hour." She knew she'd be a while because her run always turned into a walk near the end, especially when nature captured her attention.

"You have a lovely, figure, dear. You've no need to worry about losing weight, pretty thing like you. Even as tall as you are, some man will find you attractive," Ethel said, walking with Vivian down the tall staircase and onto the veranda where she settled in her rocker on the front porch of the aged Victorian house overlooking the water.

Vivian thanked Ethel again for the map and jogged down the steps to begin her run. She ran along the narrow road, cranking the music while admiring the view. Feeling the breath of a breeze on her face and the taste of salt in the air, she lengthened her stride. *The smell is amazing. Fresh, clean and ageless. God, this is just what I needed.*

She passed a small marina and with sailing boats in the water. Vivian didn't know a schooner from a yacht, but she enjoyed watching them skim over the mirror-like surface.

Beads of sweat trickled down her cheeks. The runner's high of endorphins raced through her veins, waylaying any jet leg crash. Exhilaration spurred her on, feeling excited and free. *Free to just be myself.* There was freedom in the anonymity of travelling alone.

Reaching into her arm-band holder, she cranked the music louder. *Mother would certainly frown if she heard me listening to racy dance music. That would never do. She would only think, yet again, that I am a child who is unwilling to grow up and act my age. I tried to be conservative like her and tried to be what her society expected of me. But I'm not that person and never will be. I want to be wild and run free, barefoot even, and be who I am on the inside. Time for an identity readjustment—a phrase for the thirty-something, unmarried women who weren't quite sure of their path.*

Winded, Vivian slowed her pace to a walk, changing course from the track she had been following to a trail leading to the rocky beach. Music still played strong in her ears as she walked along the uneven ground. She admired the lapping water and the houses in the distance that looked like a painted picture on a Monet across the harbour. The wharf was up ahead and small cottages that reflected their own private get away.

Finding a large, flat rock to sit on, she tilted her face toward the last rays of the evening sun. Enjoying the sun's warmth on her skin, she bopped her head, singing along with the music as sweat poured down her face and neck.

On her stride back to the lodging, she would switch to an audio book. Listening to a good book on tape was part of her cool down method, but for just a few minutes more she would continue to enjoy the heavy base rock and pop tunes—body moving music she wanted to lose herself into.

****

Tuck stepped on the back porch of his parent's home, fitting his sun glasses over his eyes when he heard something. He paused to listen closer. Someone was singing down on the beach. He followed the sound of the female voice.

The identity of the singer couldn't be anyone he knew. Surly no one from town would perch below his parent's house to sing pop music off key. Curious, he strode to the end of the lawn and glanced over the edge, where grass turned to a rocky ledge leading to the beach. He did a double-take at the vision of the woman from the airport. That was her, no doubt about it.

There was no mistaking that long neck and the inky-black hair even more spiky than earlier today. Lowering his glasses down his nose, Tuck watched as she stretched her legs in front of her, crossing her feet at the ankles. What lovely long legs she had. She leaned back as the sun kissed her smooth skin. His fingers ached, watching her weave her fingers through her cropped hair and rubbing the sweat soaked layers from her skin. Supporting her position with one hand behind her back, she continued to lounge on the rock, as if the beach was her living room. Her head bobbed as she sang. Her feet swayed across the sand.

Tuck looked right and left. She's tonight's main attraction and she doesn't even know it. She obviously didn't realize how close the houses were to the beach, and that there was no such thing as privacy in a small town.

He recognized the song as she continued to sing, slightly off key, and he wondered if she'd give voice to the explicit parts of the song as well.

He smiled, nodding his head, completely amused. There was no doubt in his mind now, this had to be the elusive Vivian. Vivacious Vivian. The name absolutely suited her.

Her sudden move to sit up straight and view her iPod caused him to jump. The song she was listening to, along with the spell he had been under, were both over. Confident he couldn't be seen standing on the higher embankment, and shrouded by trees, Tuck returned to spying on the beautiful lady at the water's edge.

Vivian fiddled with her iPod and stretched her legs—those long legs extending and reaching in such flexible ways to set a man's imagination running wild. She saw the wooden stairs leading to the path back to the roadway. She then walked with purpose across the rocky beach toward the stairs, completely oblivious to anyone watching her. The residents along the beach knew how to be invisible to strangers during tourist season.

Tuck was amused by the minor transgression of trespassing across the lawn as Vivian scrambled up the neighbour's bank and started toward the road, ignoring the stairs down the beach for such a purpose. A bit of a wild child she was.

Young Marston walked around the edge of his house bordering Tuck's parent's property, as though he happened to be going that way. Tuck knew better. The young hound dog. The randy twenty-something kid, who considered himself a man, had probably been watching Vivian the whole time.

Tuck continued to watch from behind a large oak, shielded by the foliage of the trees. He saw Marston wind himself to approach the lovely tourist. "Hey ya," Marston said as she made to walk past.

Vivian stopped—eyes wide, as if slightly startled at being caught. Marston's eyes were fixated on her breasts. She kept her composure, popping one ear bud from her ear in a fluid, graceful motion. Vivian turned to say a polite hello to Marston. Though Tuck couldn't tell for sure, but he was almost certain the boy's eyes were exploding from their sockets, seeing Vivian's nipples pushing through the thin fabric of her damp tank top.

She had a nice body Tuck would love to see right next to his. Her breasts were ripe and full, screaming to be touched. And those nipples, Tuck wanted to run his thumb over them and watch them bud, then suckle them...

*What am I thinking!* Tuck shook his head. His mother would smack the side of his head if she caught him peeking at a woman from behind a tree as though he were a school boy. His mother would admonish him that Vivian was a guest in their house, a client, and by all accounts under their protection while in MacIntosh. A woman not to be ogled by sex-craved males.

"Whatcha listening to?" The younger boy's eyes were roaming uncontrollably. "Something good, I'd imagine."

"No, nothing special." Vivian appeared completely unaware of the audience she had drawn. "I like audio books. You know the books on tape where the narrator reads the story to you. I find them relaxing."

"You don't say." Marston grinned like an innocent child caught doing something wrong. "I'll have to download one of those and see if it works on me."

"Yeah, okay." Vivian started to walk away.

"You're not from around here." Marston attempted to halt her escape. "I can tell."

"No, I'm just visiting for a couple of weeks." Vivian glanced over her shoulder, still moving along, albeit slowly.

*Good going girl.* Tuck peered between the branches. *Don't give that boy any more attention then he deserves.*

"I'm going to learn to sail, as weird as that may sound. Well, probably not weird to you, because you live here. But, I'm going to try anyway."

"Oh, ya." Marston followed Vivian down the path. "With the MacLean's? Daniel, Nate, or Randy?"

She paused, her teeth showing briefly as she bit her bottom lip. Tuck liked those lips. Pink, not too full, but wide and full of promise. Lips that Tuck would welcome a kiss from.

"I don't know. I have only been talking with Mrs. MacLean so far."

"Oh, ya." Marston continued to follow her toward the road.

Tuck could sense Vivian's nervousness as she glanced around her surroundings and her fingers curled to fists. She was looking for an escape.

Time to save her from the village idiot. Tuck strode, with what he hoped was a casual gait, toward her.

She raised her clear green eyes to his. "Hello." Her voice whispered relief.

"Ms. Mitchell?" Tuck extended his hand. He nodded at Marston, receiving a dirty look in return. "I'm Tuck MacLean. I missed you at the airport." He strived to appear smooth, tucking his thumbs loosely in the front pockets of his pants. "Dad got mixed up on the plaque card and I thought I was looking for a Margaret, not a Vivian."

"Oh." She shook his outstretched hand.

For as much as Vivian's pointed buds deserved attention, unlike Marston—junior leach that he was, Tuck kept his eyes levelled on hers. Holding her hand, he studied her face to see if she recognized him from the airport. His heart sank unexpectedly as he registered her frown in confirmation of his identity. *Shit, she probably remembered my lame-ass remark about her height.*

She released his hand to twine hers together in front of her. Her lovely eyes went cool and her face scrunched. "Yes, I recall bumping into you."

Though Tuck's father made a mistake on the plaque card, Tuck's mother insisted they make up for the error by ensuring Vivian was treated extra special when she arrived for her first lesson. Tuck had been on his way to the flower shop and then the Mariner's Roost, prior to being side-tracked by her singing on the beach. The general plan was to ply her with flowers and uncompromising maritime hospitality. His ma thought the flowers would be a nice touch.

Unperturbed by her cold gaze, Tuck forced his best smile. "My mother has no patience for blunders. Our clients are top priority. Ma likes everything perfectly arranged and the organization to run smoothly. Unfortunately, we live by the sea with a business dependent on the whims of Mother Nature, so business for us seldom runs without a setback. We apologize for the mistake at the airport and hope to make it up to you."

\*\*\*\*

Vivian forced a smile. "Your mother sounds lovely. I am looking forward to meeting her tomorrow."

Tuck glanced over his shoulder. "She's already

anticipating meeting you."

Vivian followed his stare to a blue wood-sided house with three gables. "Is this your house?"

"Oh, no." He shook his head. "This is home base. Ma runs the business outta here. My father operates the actual tours on the family dock." Tuck laughed. "I keep expecting her to come marching around the corner at any moment."

"Oh, I'm sorry. I guess I shouldn't be walking across the lawn." Feeling out of her comfort zone, Vivian squeezed her hands tight. *Damn, this was not the first impression I had hoped to portray.*

"Hey, we're a small town." He waved his hand to dismiss her concern. "The ground is for walking, and the sea is for sailing. That's why you're here, right?"

"Yes." She kicked a rock back into the landscaping before lifting her gaze to Tuck, liking that she had to look up to meet his eyes. "To be honest though, I don't remember seeing you at the airport…outside of bumping into you at the phone booth." She didn't voice that if she had she seen his face in a crowd, she would have remembered it. That square jaw, slightly ruddy cheeks, with just a mist of five o'clock shadow, and those eyes—wow. Even wearing glasses, as he was now, she could still make out their stormy depths that sent a shiver straight down her backbone. *Yes, I would definitely notice him in a crowd.*

So much for the eighteen-year old she imagined getting reprimanded by Lynette. This was no kid standing in front of her. This solid mass of rugged hardness was all man. She could barely maintain a conversation when her breath seemed lost just by making contact with those stormy eyes.

"You may not have noticed me with the sign in front of my nose." His smile revealed a full deck of pearly whites. "But you're here now. So all's well that ends well. Can I walk you back to the Roost?"

"Thanks, but no. I'm fine. I think I'll pick up the pace again." With his nearness making her jittery, she was eager to escape. "I told Ethel, she the owner of the Mariner's Roost..." His grinned caused a flush of warmth over her cheeks. "But of course, you probably already know that." She paused again to catch her suddenly missing breath. "I told her I would only be an hour and she's holding dinner."

As she turned to go, his hand touched her arm. "It's a pleasure to meet you, Vivian."

Vivian glanced from his face to his hand on her arm before returning to meet his eyes. His feathered touched caressed her skin. "It's nice to meet you, too." Quelling her melting insides at just beholding this handsome rouge of a man, she held her hand out in a departure shake. Was it her imagination or did he hold her hand a fraction too long?

"Firm grip." Tuck smiled, letting go of her hand.

This man sure knows how to douse a good mood. "Tall with a firm grip. Don't get many of us in these parts do you?" She raised a brow before turning away, placing the ear buds back in place.

"None, like you." Marston, for whom she had forgotten was there, stepped forward to hold out his hand. "Marston Miles, nice to meet you."

Vivian shook his hand, and then quickly waved at them both as she turned to leave. She wanted to look over her shoulder for one last glance at the handsome Tuck, but knew that would be too obvious.

\*\*\*\*

Marston stood beside Tuck, watching Vivian run. "Hoo, ahh." He showed Tuck a thumbs-up. "Just the sight of that curved and luscious roundness tips me into over-drive. What a piece!"

"Go home, you little punk." Tuck shook his head, no remorse for the younger man. He despised Marston since he was a wee lad, climbing up the family tree to piss on a cat. To Tuck, Marston's actions were worse than being sprayed by a skunk—for the cat and him too, since he had to wash the cat. "Ever try to bathe a cat?"

"Hey, when ya gonna get over that? I was a kid for Christ's sake."

Tuck didn't bother responding. He turned on his heel and headed for his SUV, thinking of Vivian and wondering why she seemed to be stuck in his thoughts.

\*\*\*\*

Vivian second guessed everything from coming here to what would have happened if she hadn't came as she soaked in the claw-foot tub that evening in her, oh-so-beautiful room. Staring at the dormer window, now shuttered for the evening, her emotions were like a yo-yo since setting foot on the plane this morning. One moment as high as a kite, flying with happiness and freedom that she was doing something on her own—to plummeting back to Earth, convinced she was the biggest looser for having no one to share her life with.

She was accustom to small towns, living in rural farm country like she did, but she soon learned the definite difference between small town and rural. Her little cottage sat on a small parcel of land completely surrounded by homesteads, and people tended to keep their distance unless they knew you, and even then your space was your own. After only a few hours in this town, she could tell it was similar to what her authors wrote about—people wanting to know you and get to know you. They were bold and friendly, which made her shy and apprehensive to their forward ways, yet she hope she they wouldn't make the wrong assumption. She didn't want to give off the wrong impression. Anxiety swirled in Vivian's stomach as she soaked in the tub.

Vivian wrapped a large, fluffy towel around her and pulled out her nightdress from the luggage bag. She then called Marcy to let her know she had arrived. "Well, take it for what it is," Marcy said. "It's all part of the adventure."

"I suppose. Yeah, I guess, you're right. Vivian knew she had to open up to the experience. While believing she should live the way others thought to be right, she lost herself in the process. Something as essential as to who she is—who she needs to be.

Marcy laughed. "Of course I'm right. I am a mom of two boys."

She said goodbye to her friend before crawling between the Egyptian cotton sheets, so crisp and clean. *Heavenly*.

Chapter Five

The smell of bacon wafted under the closed door, announcing breakfast the next morning. Ethel greeted Vivian with a plate piled high with the fluffiest scrambled eggs she had ever laid eyes upon, or taste buds, with a side of homemade hash browns. Thick-cut toast in wedges diamonded the platter. The scent of Lilac mixed with the aroma of breakfast, lured Vivian's eyes to a large bouquet of flowers. The beautiful native flowers were full of color and fragrance.

Vivian smiled at the lovely set table. "Oh, they're beautiful." With both hands hovering at the end of the bouquet, she thrust her face into the blooms to inhale their perfume.

"The MacLean's sent them," Ethel said, pausing to lift a hand to pat her perfect bun at the base junction of her neck and spine. "Apparently Lynette feels bad about the mix-up yesterday. Seems you and Tucker missed one another at the airport. Anyway, Billy brought them around this morning."

Touched by the gesture, Vivian buried her nose back in the flowers. "Tucker? Billy?"

Ethel's hands returned to her side, brushing the flour from her skirt. "Tucker, he likes to be called Tuck, he's Lynette's son, and Billy, is one of Daniel's boys, Randy's brother."

Vivian reluctantly left the bouquet to take a seat at

the table, wondering if Ethel would join her or continue to hover.

"You know Lynette?" Ethel's brow rose.

Vivian nodded as Ethel gave her the scoop on the MacLean's. "Lynette is married to Randy MacLean. Tucker and Nathaniel are their boys. Tucker ran off to be some big shot, while Nathaniel stayed and married that pretty Emily from down the harbor. They have two kids now. Lynette quite likes being a grandmother."

As Ethel paused in thought, though her face did not change expression and her eyes never wavered, Vivian scooped a heaping helping of eggs on her fork, and savored the flavor. *Delicious.*

"Maria and Matthew, those are the names of the kids. Almost escaped me for a moment or two. They're named after Lynette's folks. Daniel is Randy's brother and he has four children, Billy being the youngest. All except Tucker, they all work one way or another in the family business, but now the big shot is back. Taken down a notch or two he is, if you ask me and rightly so. His folks have him working in the business, seems there's always a spot for one more."

Ethel wiped her hands on the dish cloth and then tossed it on the sink's ledge. Vivian pulled a chair out for Ethel to begin her breakfast, but she wasn't done her story.

"They say Tuck has some talent. He did make me some brochures and put the Inn on that spider's web. You know that computer place."

About to correct the older woman who seemed out of touch with the modern age, Vivian changed her mind. Trying to educate the matron on the World Wide Web would be a lost cause. Interested though she may be in the information she gleaned from Ethel, Vivian was eager to meet Lynette and didn't want to be jaded in a first impression. Taking a different tact, she changed the subject. "Do you have any other guests staying with you?"

"Oh, yes, I have the Parsons, the Matthews, the Jordans, and of course, you. Typically, there are four new couple's every two weeks, but you being a single means there's just seven guests this go round. I must say I'm grateful to the MacLean's business as it keeps my Inn running. But you slept later than the rest today and they've already left to see the sights."

Vivian's gaze flicked to her tasty breakfast as it turned cold while she continued to listen to Ethel's rant.

"Lynette and I make sure everyone is well equipped with maps and such to go off exploring, but we just didn't know what to do with you, travelling by yourself and all. It's not like one of those couples could to take you along and it seemed wrong to book any tours for a single. Well, we just didn't know what to do."

Never feeling as alone as she did at that moment, Vivian forced what she hoped was a pleasant smile. Obviously Ethel thought Vivian to be some sort of defect travelling alone. Perhaps the modern woman didn't exist in MacIntosh?

"Well." Vivian sighed and folded her napkin. Having suddenly lost her appetite, she rose from her chair, "I don't want to keep everyone, being that I overslept. I'll find my own way over to the MacLean's."

"Billy said to tell you to drop by the house and Lynette would take you to the warehouse for a tour,"

Ethel said as Vivian left the kitchen.

**** 

His mother fussed about the kitchen giving orders and writing notes on her to-do list. "You'll take Vivian to the warehouse today and then show her some of the sights." Lynette turned to Tuck before leaving to begin her errands. "I should be here when she comes by though, as I don't expect to be too long."

"Much as I would love to play tour guide, Ma, I can't." He held up a finger before his mother uttered another word. "One, it's not part of my job description, despite how often you want to change it on your own whim." He held up a second finger. "And two, I have a mountain of work to get to and unless you have another IT fella on the side, I guess, I'm your man to get that done." Booking no further conversation, he headed downstairs to the office.

"It's nothing that can't wait, can it?" His mother followed him to the stairs. "She's all by herself for heaven's sake. I feel bad for her. She sounded like such a nice lady on the phone and I want her to have a good time. I can't ask Nate, it's not right with him being married. You're not married." Leave it to his mother to state the obvious. "You go."

"She's a big girl, Ma. Someone who obviously didn't need her hand held to get here and would likely resent it anyway if I offered."

"Listen here, Tucker Michael MacLean."

*Oh, no, I'm in trouble now if she's pulling out my full name.*

"Whatever you have to do can wait. Clients are important. You have making up to do for yesterday, so you'll find the time to show her around."

"Ma, she booked the trip on her own."

"Don't you sass me." She pointed a finger at him, her other hand wrapped tight around the purse slung over her shoulder.

"Ma, I'm not seven. All I'm saying is she chartered the trip. She went to the effort of finding us on-line and booked a two-week holiday that included learning the skills necessary to sail as part of a crew. We always schedule enough free time before and after to accommodate the necessity for site-seeing and the boat trip. I'm sure she can manage."

His mother's face softened into a smile, and he knew he had lost the battle. "Just offer, okay? If she says no, fine. You're off the hook. But make the offer to show her around."

Tuck sighed, holding up his hands in surrender. "Fine, you win." He continued down the stairs. "Suppose I'll have to foot the bill for this too," he mumbled. "Flowers weren't enough…"

"What's that?"

"Nothing, Ma, nothing. See you later."

Tuck didn't think he had to be a companion simply because Vivian didn't bring one. *All this fuss for some woman who came alone.* Spending unnecessary cash was no longer part of Tuck vernacular. "No one else gets this kind of treatment." He argued plaintively for his own hearing.

"Did you say something?" his mother called from the top of the stairs. When he didn't answer, he heard her footsteps move toward the kitchen door. "See you in just a bit."

Tuck heard the squeak of the door as his mother left the house. His computer monitor binged, announcing more e-mail. No longer interested in conquering the mountain of paperwork on his desk, he stood, leaning his hands on the mahogany table, letting his head swing between his shoulder blades. The descending silence reminded him of the one project he wanted to get done while the house was deserted. He shook his head, welcoming the excuse to do something besides sit at his computer. Taking the stairs two at a time, he went outside and into the garage to grab his tool belt.

The proximity of the kitchen door to the flight of stairs to his office echoed the sounds of the coming and goings of everyone through the stairwell. It wasn't so much the constant banging of the screen door that irked his nerves as the squeaking that sounded like bagpipes on their initial sigh when the kitchen door opened. While motivated he might as well take care of the banging.

The old family house was a parcel of additions. It had been added to with each generation of MacLean's living in it. His generation had just finished modifying, renovating, and expanding the old home to include offices in the basement for the business.

Many, many years ago, Old Captain MacLean, the original, did all his business from his ship or in the Tavern. Back then, business was completed anywhere from the wharf to the kitchen table, never ironically enough in the actual warehouse where the ships were built, restored, and repaired. Upon Tuck's re-entry to the business, his family had discussed building a loft in the warehouse for offices and such, but his mother was so use to working at the kitchen table, directing family traffic, and taking care of family members that she couldn't get everything done from the warehouse—so far away.

So far away…just down the road. "Not even a five-minute walk," he muttered, pushing the garage door open with his shoulder. Even this door had a mind of its own, loose in the winter allowing drafts and powdery snow to seep inside, and in the warmer weather it stuck. Inside the garage he continued his internal rant. *Comply with the boss.* He rolled his eyes heavenward, praying for patience. Though his father ran the company, he left all the details to his wife and from there she delegated. It seemed his father's main objective was keeping Lynette happy, and he and his brother, Nate, followed suit.

The rusted toolbox banged against his leg when he retraced his steps back to the porch. No matter how much grease was applied the damned thing continued to squeak. Tuck decided new hinges were in order. Even that small task wouldn't be easy because they had to have the right *look*.

"We're a sea faring family," his mother once said. "Tourists come to see us and should be pleased by what they see. Taken back in time as it were. We can't have hinges like the regular ones they sell on the shelves." She admonished him when Tuck laid the hardware on the counter the first time he attempted to do this job.

Tuck had fished the receipt out of his pocket. "Ma, I'm sure when the house was originally built, Ole' Captain' MacLean bought supplies at the local mercantile." Tuck argued fruitlessly, but knew he would be taking the hinges back

Putting the new hinges back in the hardware bag, his mother smiled, a slight twinkle to her eye causing laugh lines across her beautiful cheeks. "That's just it, and so they should look just like what he would have purchased off the shelf in the eighteen century."

The manufactured sign of straining hinges greeted his ears as he opened the back door. Convinced there were no screen doors until the middle to late nineteenth century, he opened the box that arrived yesterday, containing the hardware he had found on the internet. Expensive, but matching the historical hinges even Ole' Captain MacLean would have purchased.

Only the sound of the ocean lapping and the occasional dog barking marred the silence surrounding Tuck as worked on the door. He smiled, knowing he was fixing an historical landmark. There were several older homes in the town of MacIntosh, but the MacLean home had always belonged to a family member in one way or another. The house held many lifetimes of fond memories. The front porch, where his mom and dad sat on their favorite swing in the evenings and greeted the neighbors. The veranda on the back of the house overlooked an acre of pristine property edged by the sea. The kids always loved the lookout window in the in the attic, complete with a spyglass where they could view ships of all shapes and sizes in the far distance.

Tuck didn't know a lot about architecture, but in town they referred to the MacLean house as a Captain's House for that is exactly what it had been in the eighteenth century, a captain's house built for a ship's captain.

Great, great, however many times it took to go back to Grandpa MacLean to get to the right generational gap, was by all accounts the original sea captain. Gerald MacLean crossed the pond from Scotland in the eighteenth century. He set sail, brought along his men and their families for a fresh start away from English rule. Here, life began anew for this branch of the MacLean's on this side of the Atlantic aptly named New Scotland at the time, now Nova Scotia.

Being true to your roots only went so far with Tuck. Nothing would convince him that having to pay twice as much for a set of hinges and having them shipped across the country was worth it. A little over the top, but if it pleased his mother, so be it.

A warm day, the sun shone directly on Tuck's back. A trickle of sweat danced off the tip of his nose, He sat back on his haunches and reached in his shirt pocket for the old-fashioned hankie, wiping the sweat from his brow. He slipped it back into his pocket and grabbed for a screwdriver, cursing when it slipped from his sweaty hands.

Even while focused on his task, he couldn't miss the scent of coconuts and pina coladas as it sailed up his nose. Directly beside the ancient toolbox, a set of candy apple red toes suddenly appeared. *Huhh*. Tuck's gaze followed the cute toes, to the flawless skin on the long legs that seemed to go on forever. He stretched from his crouch position to stand upright. *Sparkling*. Her arms and legs had some sort of glitter coating them, making the reflecting light sparkle over her skin in the sunlight. He inhaled her scent. *An inviting tropical beach*.

Tuck's gaze continued to her almond shaped, sea green eyes which were staring at him, questioningly.

"Good morning, Tuck," Vivian said. Her low toned, husky voice seemed to be more suited to a late night radio talk show than a morning greeting. "Is your mother at home? I want to thank her for the flowers. They were lovely."

"Ah, what? No. I'm glad you liked them." Tuck gripped the screwdriver tightly in his left hand, completely baffled as to why he seemed a loss for appropriate conversation every time he encountered this woman. He took a deep breath. "Ma went to run some errands. She told me to tell you she'll be back in just a bit, if you want to come in and wait."

"Oh, no, I don't want to be any trouble." Vivian turned to walk away.

He didn't want her to leave. Acting before thinking, Tuck quickly rubbed his free palm along his trousers before placing it to rest on her arm, just as she was about to leave. He had seen beautiful women before. Hell, he married the original trophy wife. But with Vivian, he seemed to be tongue-tied and at a loss for sensibility, which wasn't like him. He hadn't been at a loss for words since a girl in eighth grade let him see her boobs.

"You're no trouble. My mother wanted to meet you in person and show you around." Tuck dropped his tools back in the box, hoping to cover his discomposure. "Come inside and I'll put the kettle on for some tea."

"Tea would be nice. Thank you." Vivian stepped over his tools as he held the door wide for her to enter the kitchen. "Your house is beautiful. It's just what I would expect in a fishing community. I love the red door, by the way. I did notice yesterday that many of the homes paint their doors rather vividly. I saw purple and yellow. I will have to think about something like that for my place."

With her back to him, Tuck breathed deeply, trying to identify the flavor of her scent. "I don't know how it started. The door painting, I mean, but it is different." He closed the door, and then opened it again, testing the new hinges. "This isn't my house, though. Well, not any more. I grew up here." Tuck coughed to cover his babbling. "My mother doesn't want the original nature of the house ruined with anything too modern looking, which is why I was cursing those hinges on the screen door."

"Oh, she's right." Her hands linked together as she glanced around the kitchen. "I live in an aged cottage myself, which was an original 1929 farmstead. Nowhere near as old as this home and about a fifth of the size. But I love it just the same. It's not just the character, it's the feel and the spirit of the house. My cottage is homey and this house has the same atmosphere. A family home."

"Would you like a tour?" *What? Did I really just offer to show her around?* His tongue spoke before his brain had a chance to catch up.

"I would love a tour. But are you sure? You seem busy." She pointed to the tools and hardware scattered on the floor.

"Ma would love for me to show the place off." Forgetting about the tea, he led the way out of the kitchen to the rest of the house. "My mother is very proud of the house."

"She should be."

After Vivian ohhed and ahhed over every detail, noticing the smallest of things like the knobs on the counters. Tuck guided her to the basement. He wanted to show her there was more to the MacLean's than being ancient mariners.

"How did you manage to create this space?" Vivian waved her hand around the developed office space.

He was unaccountably pleased with her reaction as though it were a direct reflection on him. Tuck noticed how genuinely wide-eyed she appeared to be over the room, which resembled a modern day office you would see in a high rise professional building. It was hard to believe with all of the natural light from the large windows that they were in a basement.

"It took some doing." Tuck smiled with pride. The transformation had been his idea. He had a client in the city that renovated his Victorian home to add a dental office. "We had to lift the house, which was quite a process, and pour a deeper basement as these old places just had cellars. Once that was done, the rest was candy."

"Candy, eh?"

He noticed how her full lips formed an appreciative smile that lit her whole face. She was attractive, but when she smiled to reveal the white perfect teeth, her whole face blossomed. Beautiful turned gorgeous with her emotions worn expressively on her face.

"Candy." Tuck leaning closer to her as the smell of coconuts filled his senses. The spell broke when the kitchen door opened. He smiled and pointed upwards.

"The door," he said by way of explanation when Vivian raised her brows. "No squeak, no slam." Tuck placed his hands on his hips. "I'm the family computer geek, so I love it when I am able to show the macho men of the family that I too have trade talent. I may not be a ship builder or a master craftsman, but I have just

proven I can, when the need arises, fix a squeaky door."
He held his hand out toward the staircase. "My mother
will be anxious to meet you."

She nodded and climbed the stairs in front of him,
delicate fingers holding the railing.

Tuck's mother approached them with a bounce in
her step. She took Vivian's hands in hers, staring into
the woman's earnest face. She then embraced Vivian in
an affectionate hug as though they had known each
other forever. "Well now, you're well matched for my
Tucker there, aren't you? So tall and beautiful."

Tuck braced for Vivian to react to the sore spot on
her height.

His mother smiled. "And here I thought I was the
only one to grow 'em tall. Your ma must love her tall
weeds as well."

Vivian laughed. A tinkle of merriment filled the
room as she leaned and returned his mother's embrace.

Stepping back from Vivian, but still retaining hold
of one of her hands, his mother turned to him. Her eyes
danced with mischief. "Thought you were busy with
mountains or something."

Damn that woman, she doesn't miss anything.
"Mole hills, as it turns out." He walked to the sink to
fill the kettle. "Notice the door?"

"I did." His mother ushered Vivian to the table, and
pulled out her biscuit tin, laying the table with tea
treats.

He turned the gas stove on under the kettle and
reached for the teacups and saucers. Tuck glanced over
his shoulder, raising a brow at his mother. "Better?"

"Much better." She smiled and took a seat opposite
Vivian. Still with an unmistakable glint in her eye, she

placed her elbows on the table. "Can you ask the new master tradesmen how he fixed his outside water pipe?"

With laughs and a good story, the visit began. As most guests did, Vivian too had fallen under his mother's spell of making people feel at home and welcomed. The smile on her beautiful face proved his assumption was correct.

****

The kettle screeched and Tuck, who had been leaning casually against the counter defending his meager trade skills, moved to the stove to pour the hot water into a teapot. Vivian quickly became absorbed in the warmth emitted by son and mother until Tuck turned from the stove, frowning.

"Guess I did too good a job of the door. All manner of creatures can come and go as they please now and we'll never hear them," he said.

Vivian turned in her chair, following the direction of Tuck's stare.

"Oh, go on with you now." Lynette scolded her son. "Marston, dear, come round and meet Vivian. She'll be sailing with us this trip. Marston is our neighbor. I use to watch him when he was little. Tucker, you grab another cup now will you?"

Vivian nodded at the gangly youth. "We met yesterday."

Marston didn't move, just stood next to her, eager and hungry eyes focused on her.

Tuck hip-bumped Marston out of the way to lay the tea tray on the table. "Are you sitting?"

"Ah…what?" Marston stuttered. "Ah…ya."

"Then sit."

"Don't mind those two." Lynette waved her hands

at the two men before pouring the tea and handing a cup to Vivian. "Never did get along. You would think they would get over past arguments."

Vivian lifted the cup to her lips to hide her smile. She could almost smell the raging hormones from the young man with hair flopped over one eye and an earring in each ear. Tuck held Marston in a dirty stare.

"Mmm, this tea is spectacular." Vivian returned her full attention to the older lady dressed in a black tracksuit as though she had just returned from the gym. "What's the brand? I have a little café and I'm always on the hunt for new menu items."

From one conversation to another Vivian and Lynette talked lively about a manner of things from Vivian's café, to boat building, to travel, and so much more. She couldn't recall the last time she was so instantly comfortable with someone. Reaching across the table she patted Lynette's hand. "I feel as though I've known you my whole life."

"I know exactly what you mean." Lynette smiled warmly, refilling their cups.

"She has that affect on everyone." Tuck kissed his mother's forehead. "It's her gift."

Vivian was touched by the natural affection. "It's a good gift. You have a beautiful home…"

"Cumm, cahumm." Marston seemed to be clearing a whole frog from his throat to be noticed.

"You work here too, Marston?" Vivian shifted in her chair to include him in the conversation.

"Ahhh…" Marston began, but was cut off by Tuck.

"No. Marston does not work here. He works down at the local tavern. Bussing tables is it?"

"Bouncing." Marston corrected, throwing his

shoulders back, trying to expand his chest in a powerful position, which was in contrast to his hands daintily holding the china cup.

The glare in Tuck's eyes clearly showed he didn't think the boy could bounce a bug, let alone any of the people who frequented the tavern.

"Tuck, given your schedule..." Her words hung momentarily in air as Lynette wrapped her hands around her teacup. "As Marston works evenings perhaps he would be kind enough to show Vivian around." She smiled at Tuck with unspoken communication.

"W...what?" Tuck stood straight.

"Oh, no." Vivian jumped up from her chair. The thought of having to trail after this creepy, ogling boy made her skin crawl. "I have a car now and able to go exploring on my own. But thank you for the offer."

"You have a car?" Marston blurted. "What kind?"

"Tell you what..." Tuck cut in over Marston again, causing huffing and returned nasty stares at Tuck from the younger man. "I just have to wait for Dad to finish his tour, and then I would love to show you some of the sights, some stuff that's not on the map. A bit of an adventure or an off the beaten track tour, if you were. I'll have Agnes put together a picnic and we can enjoy the day. Unlike the other MacLean's, frolicking on the water all day, I'm usually holed up in the dungeon."

"I'm available now," Marston said, standing up so quickly the chair fell over behind him. "No need to wait."

Vivian glanced around the table at the expectant faces. "Oh, I couldn't." She inhaled a deep breath. She wanted Tuck to be her tour guide, not Marston. Then a sudden thought struck her, who was Agnes? "Really, Tuck, I don't want your wife, Agnes, going to any trouble."

Lynette laughed. "Tuck, married? Oh, once, but that didn't last, praise God." She lifted her hands in the air. "As bad as that marriage was, we were all grateful when it ended." His mother continued. "How we have tried to hook him up with some nice girls ever since, but no luck."

Vivian chanced a look at Tuck to where he sat at the end of the table. She sympathized with Tuck's mortification. His face, previously animated, was a solid unmoving mask, and his eyes stared out the window in a glazed fashion as Lynette prattled on.

"Nathaniel has a beautiful wife and two kids, my grandkids. The nicest you'll ever meet. Agnes is the housekeeper. She's been with us for years. But listen to me going on and on."

"Yes." Tuck shook his head. "Too much information, mother."

Lynnette turned to her son, her cheeks flushing. The older woman drew an audible breath as if she realized she had been jabbering. She turned back to Vivian. "I insist you go with Tuck and have a good time."

Chapter Six

When Vivian had been preparing for her trip, she did what every single, independent woman embarking on an adventure would do—she went shopping. She had searched, scanned, and researched what to wear while sailing. It was important to get the wardrobe first. Once she had the look down everything else would follow. She considered her options. White bottoms, or solid colors like a navy blue. Would it be capris, shorts, or a skort? A striped top, preferably blue or red, complimented by a trendy scarf, if one can be managed, topped with hat and completed with boat shoes. White rubber-soled shoes, no socks. Today, she wore a dark blue polo shirt edged in white piping with her white skort and open-toed sandals.

Randy turned out to be completely adorable. He looked like an ancient hippy. Tall, perhaps the same height as his son, but thinner than Tuck, who was broader, more barrel-like across the chest. Randy's air of friendliness matched his wife.

"Young lady," he said as he showed her around the wharf. "I'm Randy today, but call me Captain MacLean when we are aboard the ship. Captain for short will suffice.

She could tell where Tuck got that easy gait of his. Randy was easy to like, almost completely grey with a bushy beard that belied the existence of any lips with a ready grin. Vivian was sure if he saw a hurricane on the horizon, it wouldn't faze him one bit. Randy would probably take charge and lead people without them even knowing they were being led to safety. He and Lynette were two peas in a pod.

Taking his leave, Randy left the administration of going through the schedule and expectations to Nathaniel, who preferred to be called Nate. He, on the other hand, was all business. He and Tuck were similar in appearance, but had different personalities. Being a strong arm in his approach, Nate cautioned the guests that although they would be sailing with experienced men, everyone would be expected to pull their weight and do their part. "I know you have all paid for the experience, but safety is the name of the game when we're out at sea. Expect the unexpected as it were. Pay attention, follow our instruction, be prepared, and most important…enjoy yourselves."

Seven would-be sailors gathered in the warehouse. Ethel had already provided Vivian with their names, but this was the first time she had an opportunity to meet everyone. They were older couples who probably had every other kind of vacation imaginable and decided it was time to taste the sea. The couples seemed rather nice, and maybe a little mistrustful of the lone woman. The women were prissier than Vivian expected. She would guess it was likely the men doing most of the sailing while their wives chatted, but she remembered to not judge, for they probably wondered about her as well.

As a group, they would start tomorrow morning on the schooner moored off the wharf, working lines, learning knots, and the general terminology of sailing.

Vivian placed her hand flat across her stomach, feeling the butterflies dance. She glanced around at the couples. They could lean on one another, but she had no one. The butterflies stopped.

Intense in his address, Nate made her question her motivation in pursuing the adventure. *Can I really do this?* She hoped so. She definitely didn't want to look like a fool.

Vivian was the last to file out of the warehouse after the couples had left. Randy, who had been scraping barnacles from the hull of a small boat, approached her. "Aghh, that's a younger man's job for sure." He laughed, causing his bushy beard to gyrate. He stepped in beside Vivian. "I'll walk you back to the house."

"Thank you. I would like that."

"Don't you worry 'bout a thing," he said, as if sensing her nervousness. "You'll catch on right fine, you will. We've had some real doozies come through here and if we can teach *them* the basics of sailing, I am quite sure you will do just fine." He tapped her shoulder. "I understand our Tuck will be showing you the sights this afternoon."

"Yes." Heat rose to her cheeks, despite her will to remain composed.

Randy took no notice of her discomposure. "Get him to take you to the Old Water Wheel. It may not look like much, but it's the best seafood around."

"Oh, Tuck is having Agnes prepare a lunch, but I don't want to be any trouble." Just thinking about spending the afternoon with a sexy man, who looked exactly as she imagined a man born of the sea, caused goose bumps to tickle her arms. His straight brows, clear eyes, and powerful build represented a man use to being in charge. Relief filled her when she heard he was single.

"Phhh." Randy's gravelly voiced retuned her attention. "That's lunch. I'm talking a nice supper."

"I'm sure Ethel…" The words died on her lips as she spotted Tuck striding toward them. He wore a blue striped shirt, casually opened at the collar and the sleeves rolled to just above the elbows. *Computer techie maybe, but definitely not a geek.* Vivian's eyes were drawn to him like a magnet despite her best effort to ignore the pull he seemed to exude. *Abercrombie and Fitch beware. Here's your next poster boy.*

When he saw her, his easy smile drew her closer still. Dazzling white teeth sheathed behind lips she wanted to bite. *Where did that come from?*

"There you are." Tuck handed her a motorcycle helmet.

"You seem to be in good hands." Randy gently patted her hand and continued walking toward the porch. "Tuck, I told her you would take her to the Old Wagon Wheel." He glanced over his shoulder. "Don't let me down, son." He gave his son a meaningful look before winking at Vivian.

****

After his father went inside the house, Tuck turned to Vivian, her peachy skin colored a lovely pink. *Beautiful.*

"Do you ride?" He asked when Vivian seemed apprehensive of the helmet in her hands. The question and uncertainty in her green eyes spoke volumes and pulled at his heart in an unexpected way.

"I've always wanted to when I was a kid, but no, I

never did. I don't think…"

"Don't think then." Tuck smiled. "I use to think too much and you don't even want to know where that got me. Over-thinking kills all the fun."

A memory of his mother's monologue this morning about his failed marriage twisted in his gut, but he quelled the frustration knowing she didn't mean any harm, only got carried away.

"You know, you're right." Vivian nodded and plunked the helmet on her head.

Silence descended like a thick fog. Tuck tore his stare away from her mesmerizing eyes. "I'll get the bike."

She laughed, fidgeting as if nervous. "I guess that would help."

He led the way back up the drive, and lifted the bike from its stand. "Get on." He patted the seat behind him while fastening his own helmet.

\*\*\*\*

The big machine rumbled to life. Sitting so close to Tuck was invigorating and intimate. They rode down the winding coastal road passing occasional traffic in no real hurry. It was an experience unlike any other. Another first for Vivian. The bike propelled like the wind along the roads following the edge of the coastline. The turns were so sharp with their speed being just a touch faster than safe, Vivian focused on not falling off as she leaned into the bend.

A little shy and unsure at first, she hung onto the back of her seat for support.

He lifted a hand from the handlebar to point to his waist. "It'll be easier if you hang on to me."

Self conscious about wrapping her arms around a

near stranger, Vivian hesitated, but after another bend in the road, her thumping heart got the better of her and she quickly gripped Tuck's hips. With the safety of his body against hers, she was less frightened and her misgivings of bike riding were quickly swept away. Weaving back and forth on the winding road seemed to mirror the movement of the ocean.

"It's breath taking." Vivian sighed when they arrived at the end of a pier near a lighthouse. "I imagined this view so many times, but actually seeing it is totally different."

"Wait 'til you're out on the sea. Everything is different from that perspective. Rocks and crags that you climb over on land can be both a home coming and a grave yard."

Her eyes went wide. "What do you mean?"

"Take those rocks you see jutting out above the waves just beyond the pier."

Tuck pointed, and she held her hand over her eyes for shade from the sun.

"A home coming. Land ho. That sort of thing. Now imagine a stormy night. Think fog so thick you can't see your hand before your face. Freezing, pelting rain, just bone chilling. You know you're close to land, but you can't yet see it because of the fog and bam."

He cracked his fist into the palm of his hand, causing her to jump.

"You rip the hull of your vessel. Just like that and down you go. That's why lighthouses and buoy's are so important. They provide markers, indicators of dangers along the coastal line."

"But the sailors would be so close to land, surely they'd swim to shore." Raising her hand to her brow again, Vivian peered over the water to the distant, jutting rocks that now reminded her of razor blades waiting to strike

Tuck moved around the bike to remove a blanket from the back. "Nah, sailors don't swim. Shall we picnic here?"

"Yes. This would be nice." She hesitated. "They don't swim? They don't even try?"

"Oh, I'm sure when push comes to shove, they try. It's almost like a superstition. You may think sailors know how to swim, but many of them, of ages gone by and perhaps even today, can't swim. They don't want to learn how to swim."

"Why? That seems a little crazy to work the sea and not know how to protect yourself."

"It's a superstition for them. If they can't swim, the sea will take them fast. If they could swim, they would suffer."

Settling on the blanket and enjoying a fresh egg salad sandwich on thick-cut homemade bread, Vivian gazed out to sea. She pondered his words. "Can you swim?"

"Ah, yes, I can." Tuck grinned. "Somewhat."

Something cocky in his tone caught her attention. She turned to stare at his merry grey eyes. "You say that like it's a foregone conclusion."

"Sorry, it's just that swimming for me is part of me. I was—correction, trying again to be a rescue swimmer with the Coast Guard. When I was younger it paid for University. I've been away from it for a while, but now that I'm back, it'd be weird if I wasn't part of it. I'm a reservist. I have to get back in shape. I can't very well be expected to save someone who's depending on me if I can't swim fast and true."

Vivian eyes wandering down the length of his torso and to his legs, thrust out in front of him and crossed at the ankle. *He's in fine shape to me.*

As a diversion from her male starved cravings, Vivian loaded the conversation with questions on how he came to be a rescue swimmer.

He graciously answered each one. "People for the most part are complacent about the power of the sea." He finished a second sandwich. "They think a weather forecast is all they need. It drives my family, and those in sea rescue, crazy. People go out for a good time, but they forget that between wind, the ocean currents, and the power of the sun things can change in a heartbeat. Out there…" He pointed in the direction of the waves crashing on the rocks. "If you're not prepared, and even sometimes when you are prepared, bad things happen and lives are lost."

A shutter filtered down her spine. "Now you sound like Nate. That's just the kind of stuff he was talking about today. Made me wonder how I ever thought I could come to learn to sail."

"Nah. Don't question your choice. We have to through all the bad stuff first. To make sure everyone is aware of the dangers." Tuck smiled, leaning closer to her, almost as if encouraging her to move closer. Her heart somersaulted in her chest. "The rules have been drilled into us since we first took breath."

"I can imagine." She released a breath, not realizing she had been holding it.

Leaning back, Tuck grabbed his saddlebags. "On that cherry note, let's have desert."

Vivian laughed and helped him unload the bag.

During the pleasant lunch on the pier, they watched the gulls circle, calling *mine, mine, mine* in their high pitched ritual, waiting for Vivian and Tuck to leave so they could pick at any crumbs left behind. Out in the water, Vivian would often see a fin break the surface once in a while. Tuck informed her they were blue fins or tuna. He explained how the blue fins would be in season soon and the lobster season was also open. "The markets will be full this year, which means money will roll in."

"How so?"

"Don't listen to the fishermen's bellyaching. In just a few weeks, they can make what it takes most people a year to earn."

"No kidding?"

"No kidding. It's not easy money by any stretch. They certainly do work for it." Tuck popped another homemade oatmeal cookie in his mouth and brushed the crumbs off his shirt. "Sometimes money earned that fast gets lost even quicker."

"I can imagine." Vivian nibbled a delicious cookie. "Your whole family sails? No, you said you were the geek. You don't sail? You swim. Surly you sail too?"

"Thanks for the geek reference."

She laughed, pointing an accusing finger at him. "You said it. I'm just repeating."

He tilted his head back and joined her laughter. "Okay, you're forgiven, this time." He gazed at her with a teasing glint in his wide eyes. "We were all brought up on the water. You can't call yourself a MacLean if you can't handle a boat, but my interests are more land bound. Computer programming was my thing."

"Ah, so not just a wanna-be geek. You're the real thing." Vivian wanted to know what made Tuck tick. "So why, *was*?"

"I only do it for the family now. At one time I was part of a large company that went bust in the tech bubble and lost it all. Much like a fisherman, as fast as I made the money, it disappeared quicker."

"That must have been hard." She folded her napkin and placed it back in the bag.

"Let's hope you never know." He winked. "We should really change the subject. Between dying fishermen and my lost career, I'm a bit of a downer. You won't believe me if I told you I'm not usually so pessimistic." He tossed his napkin in the bag with the remaining food containers. "So, tell me all about you."

His bright smile warmed her heart as his soft grey eyes turned her insides to liquid. Biting her tongue to suppress her yearnings to nibble his lower lip, she averted her gaze. It had been far too long since she had any kind of interaction with a man and she was clearly out of practice. No one's fault but hers for hanging around married women and not getting back on the dating saddle.

"I do a few things to keep busy. Aside from the café I run with my business partner, who also happens to be my best friend, I'm a reader for a publishing house. I also have a hobby of collecting junk." Accustom to raised eye brows when she explained what she did for a living, Vivian waited for his response.

Tuck did not disappoint. "Junk?"

"My mother would farm my brothers and I off on our grandparents—my father's parents, when we were kids. She couldn't handle the stress of us."

Tuck smiled, leaning back on his elbows.

"Mother use to say…"

"Mother?" He interrupted.

"Yes, Mother. My mother considered anything less than the full word, disrespectful."

"I see," he said.

Vivian, having already fallen in love with his Ma, doubted Tuck understood. She swallowed a mouthful of water from her bottle and stared out to the deep blue ocean.

A tanned hand nudged her shoulder. "You were saying?"

Surprised that he wanted her to continue, she smiled. "Gran and Gramp's house was what Mother referred to as being full of junk and we were never, ever under any circumstances to bring any home with us."

"Your grandparents were a little less stiff?"

She laughed. "Yes. I love them dearly. And I never saw junk. It was ancient treasure to me. The clutter added to the welcome into their home. Made you feel comfortable, you know?"

"I know. Ma's a bit like that. Anything old is in."

"It's strange how something vintage can bring such comfort."

"Vintage? That's a good word for it." He glanced at her, his sunglasses mirroring her face. "So that's how you got into the junk business? Which by the way, I don't believe for one moment that the stuff you sell is junk."

"When I was twenty-one, Gran and I went to Arizona with a bunch of women on a bus tour."

"Oh?"

"Yeah, I know. Geriatric squad, right?"

"I'm picturing a bunch of clucking hens."

"Some were for sure, but I'm telling you, it was the best time I ever had."

"You don't get out much."

Vivian laughed and swatted his arm, enjoying his company. "Now, I just feel silly telling you all this."

"No, no. Please, continue." He nudged his sunglasses partway down his aquiline nose, his profile revealing a long Tom Selleck-like dimple. *Oh, I like that.* "Really, I'm riveted by a bus tour of old ladies."

With an exaggerated sigh she continued. "Anyway, Gran and I were always close, but my brothers were always around. On this trip, we really bonded..." Vivian paused, lost in the memory. "We stopped at a road-side bizarre of sorts and the women went exploring. A woman on the tour fell in love with an old ring. Blue sapphire, I will never forget it." Vivian closed her eyes, picturing the square cut ring in white gold. "An old bitty on the tour told her to put it back, that it was just road-side junk. But the woman told her friend she didn't care, plastic or not, she loved it and worth the ten dollars. It was uncommon for her to stick up for what she wanted. Well, when we returned to the hotel, she went to a local jeweler. Guess what the ring was worth?"

"A couple hundred bucks?"

"Try a couple thousand."

"Wow."

"Yeah, wow. That's when I became hooked on junk."

****

"Did your Gran ever give you the ring?" Her jaw drooped, and Tuck knew he surprised her, guessing the woman's true identity.

"Not yet, but as the only girl in the family, she told me it's mine. She wears it every day, says it reminds her of our trip and how a little luck falls on everyone. " Vivian pulled her knees to her chin and crossed her ankles, wrapping her arms around them and rocking to the rhythm of waves on the ocean. At that moment, she resembled a teenager than the siren who had been belting out rock tunes the day previous. "I think that trip is what convinced me to take some shop courses on the side. Gran supported me on that—on all of my ideas, really."

Tuck sat straight. "Whoa, wait a minute." He removed his glasses. "Shop? You took shop classes."

She grinned, like a sneaky cat that had just licked the cream when you weren't looking. "Thought that would get you." She flicked a blade of grass at him. "After we opened the café, I registered for evening classes at the local college, just some basic mechanics. Sometimes there's stuff you find that needs a little tinkering."

"Shop?" Tuck shook his head. He found it an outrageous turn on to meet a woman who understood basic mechanics.

Her head fell back as she laughed, low and husky. "Don't get the wrong idea. I'm no expert. I know enough to tinker, but I can't fix a car or anything like that."

"Me either." But he dug the idea of chick wearing a tool belt.

"According to your mother, you're slowly mastering the craft."

He shrugged, his shoulder brushing hers. He

struggled with the urge to kiss her. That sweet, innocent expression with slight pouting lips, begging to be kissed. He forced his eyes away from the temptation.

"Mother doesn't understand my obsession, of course. But because of Gran, I at least get some backing from my father."

"But it's more than junk you say. Your girl friend and you have the café as well?"

"Marcy's a classic chef and I'm a hack."

"I doubt that." Tuck interjected.

"Agree to disagree then. Our styles are different, but we both love to cook. She was professionally trained and I learned through her. She used to work in classy restaurant, but the pressure became too much."

Tuck imagined an iron chef with the intense schedule, anxiety, and close to abusive atmosphere of a high-end restaurant kitchen.

"Are you sure you want to hear this? I must be boring you."

"Yes, and not at all." He nudged her shoulder. "If I wasn't interested, trust me, I would have come up with some excuse by this point."

Vivian explained how her friend, Marcy, newly married and working her dream job, hardly ever saw her husband. "Her schedule was in total opposition to his and what started as a fairy tale career quickly changed in priority. She wanted a family and decided to try her hand at something else. Marcy was at my place one day when I was restoring a couple of old floor lamps, and the rest as they say, is history."

"Floor lamps? Please don't tell me you started a business based on floor lamps." He stretched out his legs, enjoying the summer sun on his face, and the feel of her arm beside his. "It's either the way you tell the story or something I haven't put my finger on yet, but so far I have a Safire ring and floor lamps."

"To be honest I never really thought about it like that before, but I guess you're right." She stretched her legs and leaned back on her hands. If he were a bit closer, he could cover her hand with his own.

"Marcy said if she had a restaurant of her own she would put floor lamps like the ones I had beside the tables to create a homey setting. And there you have it. That was that." She slapped her hands together.

Tuck was unconvinced. "I happen to know firsthand it takes more than a lamp to create a business."

"You're right, of course. But that's how the idea of combining a café with a nick-knack shop sprung to life. Now we operate seasonally, just off the highway between her house and mine. At first, our many critics thought no one would stop at a café close to town, but they do. And they come back. Marcy is an exceptional cook and people wait all year for the May long weekend for the café to open."

"Maybe you should have cooked our lunch." Tuck spontaneously pulling her sunglasses down her nose with the tip of his finger. "You have the most beautiful green eyes."

"Ah, thank you." Vivian gasped for a breath. "But I'm on vacation, no cooking."

Tuck turned to face her, leaning even closer to brush his lips over hers.

\*\*\*\*

An instant heat filled her core when his lips touched hers. Vivian didn't push him away. Why would she? Her heart hit the floor of her stomach, spreading tendrils of excitement coursing through her veins. His lips were like the soft caress of a feather teasing across her slightly parted lips. His thumb brushed her cheek and continued to move slowly across her ear to rest at the back of her head as he deepened the kiss, brushing his tongue across hers.

*Oh, this is what I wanted to do since first meeting Tuck.* Vivian got lost in the moment as the sea breeze brushed over her like a warm caress. His hand behind her head held her as he deftly explored her lips. His mouth was fresh and inviting, tasting like the salt sea air.

As quickly as the kiss began, it was over. He leaned back casually as though he did this kind of thing every day. Perhaps he did. Standing, he held out his hand. "We better get going. We have some ground to cover."

Her legs wobbled as she stood, but she refused his offer to help, hoping to show as little reaction to the kiss as he was. Did he take all of the tourists out and causally kiss them on the beach, rocking their world and making the angels sing, only to carry on as though nothing happened?

With hardly a word spoken on the way back, he dropped her off at the door of the Inn like a perfect gentleman.

She replayed the kiss in her mind as she paced her room. She had never been kissed like that before. Tuck's kiss made her knees weak and he what—just walked away, unfazed? Was this an everyday experience for him?

The picnic had been so lovely. They shared

memories and got to know each other. She was more comfortable with Tuck than she had ever been with another man. She connected to him.

The whole ride back, Vivian hoped he would pull over and kiss her again. How she wanted his lips on hers again, to feel that instant passion. The sensation he created in her core from the brush of his finely molded lips was completely new. But then he dropped her off at the door as chaste as a brother. Only dropping a light kiss on her cheek and telling her he would see her soon.

Vivian's hand cupped her cheek where his lips had last touched, and then let her hand fall. Soon? What did that mean? Where she came from you don't kiss and run. Her clenched hands relaxed and rested on her hips, as she walked to the window. Maybe Tuck didn't like kissing her? But a woman would know—would sense his dislike. Right?

He's obvious not into her. She should have known from his lame-ass remark at the airport. Well, it was his loss. She wouldn't be left at the door as though she were a child. She was on vacation and wanted to have some fun. It was still light outside and she wasn't going to bed yet.

Determinedly fixing her hair and makeup, Vivian decided to walk down the main street and see what the town held in the way of nightlife. She had never been one for going to bars, but this was the new Vivian and she wanted to go out and meet people. Tuck couldn't be the only good looking guy in town. If there was one, there were bound to be more.

She grabbed her purse and sweater, and walked down the stairs, tip-toeing as though she was sneaking out of her parent's house for a hot date.

## Chapter Seven

Vivian walked the entire downtown core and to her horror there seemed to be only two places to choose from for an evening drink. Seedy and seedier, otherwise referred to as the Tavern and Bullets. Each boarded the main street across from one another. She stood on the curb, eyeing them wearily and then remembered that Marston indicated he worked at the Tavern. Without further pondering, in she went.

You could have heard a pin drop when she opened the large mahogany door and entered the taproom. Javex, with a hint of left over vomit, perfumed the air as she made her way to a table in the furthest corner of the room. The men, for most of them present were men by Vivian's estimation, looked as though they had been carved from the same mahogany as the furnishings. They stood so wooden, blending in with the general decor. Only sheer will-power and bravado kept Vivian from turning tail running out. This was a small town on the Eastern Seaboard, what could possibly happen?

Platinum blond hair streaked with a bold pattern of purple and red stalked toward her table. "What can I get for you this evenin'?"

Vivian kept her purse on her lap. The squat, solidly-built woman who appeared to be in her mid fifties, and well-use to dealing with trouble, waited for an answer.

Glancing around the large, mahogany decorated interior, Vivian's mind blanked. "Ahhh."

"Nope, don't sell that here." The waitress' low-pitched words were softened by the friendly smiled she bestowed on Vivian. Truly, this woman could probably take on anything flung her way and the glare she turned to the men seated at the bar clearly indicated she had no time for bullshit. "A beer, perhaps? Whisky? Dan's not really into fancy umbrella drinks, but I can twist his arm if that's all you're use to, honey."

Beer or hard liquor? What a choice. Despite what the waitress said about the arm twisting, and Vivian was sure she could do it, she didn't have the nerve to even ponder the wrath of Dan if she asked for a margarita. Contrary to her friendly wink, Vivian was sure this waitress wouldn't think twice about tossing her out on her ass if she ordered a virgin Caesar.

"Whiskey, please. Tall glass with Ginger Ale. Thanks." Vivian smiled and the woman nodded as she stalked away, her too short shirt hugging her older curvy form.

Vivian gazed out the window, avoiding her own reflection. A quick glance revealed a face that had the appearance of someone caged. Caught in a net of her own design. She waited for her drink, desperate for something to do with her hands. She really hadn't thought this through very well. Vivian had been so frustrated by Tuck's kiss all she wanted was to get out of the close confines of her room. Space, she had needed space.

Where did Tuck learn to kiss like that? Self-proclaimed computer geeks are not suppose to even know how to kiss, let alone melt a woman in the most

94

perfect of settings, on a beach with a breeze tickling and a picnic at their feet. Who did he think he was?

"Shall I start a tab for you, hon?" Platinum was back with the drink in hand. "It'll get busy in here shortly so best to do it now before we're swamped."

"Really?"

"Oh, yeah. Friday nights the Tavern gets hopping with some local music and everyone comes by. Don't let the local color fool ya." She nodded at the men still seated at the bar who every once and awhile cast glances toward Vivian. "They just look hard. They're dandies underneath."

Vivian leaned to glance around the woman. "I'll have to take your word for it. I'm Vivian, by the way."

Pointing to her nametag housed on a sliver of fabric just above the swell of left breast, she said. "Margie. Nice to meet you." As Margie's face opened with a winning smile, Vivian noted how the genuine smile took years off her face. "You sit back and relax. You'll love the music. Everyone does."

"Okay." Vivian heard more conviction from her voice than she actually there would be.

Try as she might to drink the tall glass of liquor slowly, she downed it. The whiskey was so smooth. The amber liquid slid down her throat like warm honey, tickling her toes from the inside and making her feel fuzzy.

"You should water this down for me," Vivian suggested when Margie brought glass number three to the table.

"Don't worry. Enjoy this one. You'll be lucky to get another now that the crowd is arriving." Margie pointed over her shoulder at the band setting up in the corner.

Just as the barmaid predicted, the pub filled fast. From the moment the band struck their first note, the party was on. Dancing, laughing, shouting, and carousing erupted in the bar. Vivian soaked it in, unnoticed for once, as she sat in her corner, enjoying the evening and nursing her drink. The cover songs were dispersed with the band's originals and the crowd loved them. As drink number four arrived, Vivian sang along, letting the atmosphere engulf her.

She sat straighter, trying to focus her slightly blurred vision. She loved the sound of an acoustic guitar. The strumming of the melody melted her. *One of my all-time favorites.* Before this song, Vivian didn't bother to check out the band. She had stayed occupied with people watching, the antics of the locals providing ample amusement. But with one of her favorite songs being plucked, old style, just the way she imagined the original artist playing, she had to see who had such magic fingers.

She wandered through the crowd, toward the stage. Her breath caught in her throat. It couldn't be? *Tuck?* His eyes were closed, head slightly bent forward over the instrument as his magic fingers created harmony. Those same fingers that splayed across her cheeks and held her head as his lips brushed across hers earlier that day.

"Sing it, Tuck." A petite girl with blonde hair piled high on her head swayed in front of the stage.

Not to be out done, a rambunctious red head in platforms, wearing a tiny mini skirt and tube top yelled. "Sing it for me, Tuck."

A momentary pang of loneliness assaulted her,

realizing everyone here knew Tuck. But then of course they would. This was his home. They likely all grew up together. Vivian was the stranger. He had made her feel so special this afternoon she had forgotten she was the odd one out.

More of the crowd chimed in. "Ya, sing it Tuck!"

With a voice needing no reinforcement, Tuck complied. His head lifted slightly to acknowledge the crowd, and then he closed those beautiful sea-faring eyes and started to sing. Vivian followed suit, swept away in the story of the song.

She was lost in the midst of the lyrics, back on Tuck's motorcycle, gliding along the highway, just the two of them. As the song progressed, so did her imagination with his lips on hers, and the warmth of his hands on her body. Drink in her hand, she swayed to the rhythm of his song, absorbed in the moment. When he ended to a ruckus of applause, he opened his eyes. Like a magnet, eyes, the color of stormy skies, focused on Vivian. Her pulse quickened in anticipation as though they were the only two in the bar. He smiled, and in her mind, reinforced her crazy notion that he truly had sung the song just for her.

The crowd cheered and begged for more.

A hand touched Vivian's arm, forcing her back to earth. "You came after all," Marston said. "What'd ya think?"

"Oh, I like it," Vivian said as the band began a faster song.

Another hand shot out to hers and pulled her toward the dance floor. "You're not from around here." A beefy man, who still held her hand, started to bustle and shift his weight in some sort of dance move only he was privy to. Ham-hock hands encircled her waist, preventing her from moving in the other direction. "Finish up your drink and we'll dance."

Not knowing what else to do with the drink, Vivian did as she was bid and swallowed the remaining whiskey in the half empty glass. She shimmied to set the empty glass on the closest table and was then led back to the dance floor. Another song she knew started. Before she knew what was going on, she had another drink and a new dance partner. Each face blended, and in a small corner of her mind, it was time to call it a night and head out, but she had never had so much fun.

With a fuzzy brain, her limbs turned to liquid. She moved to the music like she had always wanted to dance—free of her cumbersome inhibitions.

Her mind danced as she swayed to a slow song with some fellow holding her drink while she sang along. *If only Tuck would play that guitar again. So sweet.*

"That's probably enough for tonight," said a thick voice in her ear. Warm fingers twisted around her wrist, and an arm folded over her shoulder as she swayed.

Lifting her head, she glanced around the near dark room. "T…Tuck?" she slurred, hearing his voice, but his face wouldn't come into view, no matter how hard she tried to focus. "I was just thinking of you. Y…you play beautifully. P…play it…again. Play another one for m…me."

"Ya, play it again, Sam." Her dance partner chimed in sarcastically with a high pitched fake voice causing Vivian to giggle.

"No, his name is n…not S…Sam," Her words slurred. "Tuck. Say it with with with me…Tu…ck."

Moving faster than she could process and slower than she wanted, Vivian vaguely processed what happened next. Raised voices, and the sound of a table crashing to the floor, pierced her ears. Margie led her to the door, at least she thought it was Margie.

"You have no head for the booze," Margie said, guiding Vivian to a bench outside. "I thought anyone who orders a whiskey and Ginger Ale knows what it does. Live and learn, as they say. We'll let the boys clear their heads while we take some air, shall we."

"O…hh." Vivian hiccupped. "O…hh…kay."

"You sit here and I'll send Tuck out when he's done."

"Dun what?" Vivian blinked to clear her vision.

Margie laughed, cupped Vivian's shoulder affectionately and went back inside.

Whatever Tuck was doing seemed to take forever. "S…so tired." Vivian laid her head on the bench to rest. She giggled as she watched the stars dance overhead.

Of a sudden, time sped up again. It seemed like a only a minute after she laid her head down, just getting comfortable on the hard bench, when a low voice echoed in her brain. "My God, really! I can't believe this. What were you thinking?" Tuck's exasperated outburst hurt her head.

"That you, Tuck?" Vivian smiled. "I…had so…much fun."

"How the hell am I going to get you back into Ethel's without all the tongues wagging? She's the biggest gossip in this town." He chastised her as he pulled her off the bench and positioned her body in the direction of the Inn.

She moved, but couldn't feel her feet as they

walked. Tuck's arm wrapped around her waist, his hand molded to her hip, holding her steady and warming her fuzzy brain. She relished the heat of his arm around her. Vivian squirmed to glance at him, noticing he wasn't wearing his glasses and had an icepack held to his forehead.

"Wh…what, happened to you…you?"

A hard face glared at her in the gloom from the street lamp. "Nothing. Just don't say a word." His apparent anger penetrated her muzzled brain.

Vivian stopped, swaying slightly, pulling out of his grip to put her hands on her hips. "Listen here, you! Don't tell me what to do. You're no boss of me."

Legs spread, Tuck removed the towel and icepack from his head. He glanced down as he carefully folded the towel, rewrapping the icepack, and again laid it against his temple. With an audible breath, only then did his hard eyes to meet hers. "I'll tell you what to do and rightly so. What were you thinking? You come to a small town and think nothing can happen to you? Everything's so safe and cozy because it's picturesque?" His breathing was labored. "You let some guy paw you all night and think he won't have any expectations? I don't know where you come from, but the girl I met this afternoon wouldn't be that stupid."

Vivian wobbled, but kept her feet in place, spread and preparing for combat. "Stupid? Girl!" She took a halting step in his direction, trying not to trip. "I'm no girl and I'm not stupid. I run my own business. I have a good career. I…"

"Stupid and naïve is what you are!" Tuck interrupted, pointing to his swollen eye. "I don't know how I'm going to explain the shiner tomorrow. I haven't had a black eye since Nate and I were in high school. Damn!" He stomped his foot in the dirt. "Man! I just can't believe this."

She moved forward, willing her body to comply. "Where did ya get the shiner?"

Tuck closed the distance between them, returning his arm around her waist. "Ohmigod." Huffing, he shook his head. "Never mind."

\*\*\*\*

Removing the icepack and towel from his face, he tossed them in a trash can, before bracing his feet and draping her left arm over his shoulders. Without another word, he propelled her up the street toward the bed and breakfast. When they got to the front gate, he stopped and let her go. "I think you'll be fine from here. Just keep quiet and maybe, just maybe, Ethel won't wake up. Though I doubt she's even asleep knowing you're out."

He shook his head as Vivian swayed from side to side as she started up the path. Then she turned and staggered back toward him. If he had been in a better mood, he would have laughed at her windup. As she strove to fit her hand on her hip to maintain her balance, he pinched his lips together to contain his hilarity.

"Y…you know, you're not the same guy who kissed me today and played guitar," she began. "Th…that guy was, wow! You on the other hand, you suck!" With all the poise of frog, she turned with a huff. Thankfully, she kept her comments to herself on the rest of the walk home.

A trickle of blood ran down his cheek. He reached in his back pocket to retrieve his handkerchief and held it to his head.

Vivian continued to wobble and sway as though she were balancing a hula-hoop. An involuntary snicker escaped him.

She turned around, almost falling into the bushes. "What?" She frowned.

*Really?* It was hard to stay mad at someone who looked so adorable when she was drunk. Her glazed eyes reflected the moonlight as she tapped her foot, waiting expectantly for his answer.

He shoved his handkerchief in his pocket and moved toward the gated path, catching Vivian before she fell. Clamping her body tight to his, he turned her around, one hand bracing her neck and the other at the small of her back. Without further thought to his actions, he bent and fastened his lips to hers.

She stiffened for a brief second and then wrapped her arms around his neck, fitting her body to his. Her mouth yielded to his onslaught, raging his emotions. He tasted the slight iron of blood mixed with her sweetened whiskey when she bit his lip. He broke the kiss, only pulling back marginally from her to stare deep into her eyes.

Beyond the haze of desire, he claimed her mouth again, hard and punishing, to make an impression.

Her arms twined tighter around his neck, drawing him closer still. Her tongue dueled with his as he pressed closer, showing her his need. His breath was ragged as he skimmed her throat and he reveled in her desire as she threw her head back, her limbs liquid to his touch. As her hands splayed across his pecks, Tuck moved his hands lower to squeeze her backside. Unwilling to relinquish control, his lips returned to hers, his tongue penetrated her mouth in an all out assault. It was a battle of passion, of which they were well matched.

Heart pounding, his lower body stiffened with the need to possess her. She leaned her head back, welcoming his touch. His hand roamed her back. He marveled how soft and desirous she was in all the right places.

"Yes." Her whisper filled his ear. "Absolutely, yes."

He moved his hands to her hips, pressing his firm member to her ensure she understood the depth of his arousal.

She took his earlobe between her teeth, flicking it with her tongue. He moaned as she rubbed against him in that ageless rhythmic motion of agreement between lovers.

A sudden whistle rang out from the trees, followed by, "You go Tuck! You show her how the local boys do it!"

Like cold water dosing a fire, he released her and moved away. "I'm sorry." His voice was hoarse and barely audible. "I got carried away."

Her eyes were unfocused. The irises dilated to dominate their depths. "What?"

Running his thumb along her swollen lips, he slid his tongue out between his own battered lips, tasting blood.

"I…" He coughed. "I have to go." *If I don't go now, I'll take you right here in Ethel's flower garden.*

She shrugged her shoulders and turned, swaying toward the front door.

Despite her awkward gait, he still wanted to haul her back into his arms, and he could have. She was in no shape to refuse. But he wasn't that type of guy. He shook his head, reaching a hand to inspect his battered lip.

The rage that consumed him when he saw Big Mike pawing her on the dance floor was a white-hot fury he had never experienced. Even when Tuck was married and men looked at his wife with carnal intent, he didn't get angry. Back then ego ruled the day, and he would think *eat your heart out fellas*. Yet tonight was different. A possessiveness had taken over. He couldn't stand the prospect of another man touching Vivian's exquisite hips, or kneading her firm, rounded backside like he had some right to it. Tuck wondered why he should care. One kiss on a pier didn't give him sole rights to Vivian, but he couldn't deny that he wanted her for himself. He had experienced an unexpected closeness with her this afternoon. Something he had never experienced with another woman.

*This is ridiculous. She's just a tourist. She isn't mine and I definitely don't believe in soul mates.*

If she wanted to get drunk in a bar and act idiotic, she would have to suffer the consequences. Why should he care? But Goddamnit, he did.

Even before he gave into his urge to kiss her this afternoon on the beach, he sensed she was special, that she was struggling to break free, but to do it on the dance floor?

Tuck had pulled Margie aside when he saw Vivian dancing. He jaw fell open when she told him Vivian was drinking whiskey.

Margie had shot him an irritated glare. "She orders, I serve. It's called a Tavern for a reason. People come here to drink. Most times to get drunk."

Before Tuck could do anything about Vivian, the crowd demanded another song. The guitar was thrust back in his hands and he was playing, craning his head to catch sight of the tall brunette with the spiky hair. Then he saw, her head back and laughing. Her long legs moved in rhythmic motion to the songs he played, and her body flowed like liquid, igniting a molten fire in the center of his being. He was mesmerized by her as if he was an ageless sailor watching the tide ebb and flow.

Playing the guitar was as easy as breathing. It was Tuck's best way to relax, and after his little tryst with Vivian this afternoon he needed to get his head in order. Stopping that kiss had been one of the hardest things he had faced in a long while, but he didn't want to take advantage of her. He decided to go to the Tavern to blow off some steam. Maybe hook up with Mary Anne and get the tourist out of his head.

Tuck and Mary Anne had a mutual agreement. Nothing serious, just a casual *as needed* relationship, and exactly what he needed to block his thought of Vivian. When Tuck walked into the Tavern and saw Mary Anne with Jared, Tuck didn't interfere. He knew Mary Anne had a real thing for Jared and he hoped it would work out for them. He liked Mary Anne and wanted her to be happy. *Happy* was something he could never give her, because he wasn't looking for a *forever* with her.

Continuing to reflect over this evening's events during his walk home, Tuck realized casual had become his motto, his style for a long time now. He wondered if he would ever be cut out for a *real* relationship after the whip-burn he received from his ex.

The pain over his left eye erased all consideration

of a serious relationship. He contemplated on how he was going to explain the black eye, that he was sure to have in the morning, to his his family. His mother would go crazy.

He was lucky to have just a shiner, and equally lucky that Big Mike fell harder than he punched. Tuck had tried verbally to let the big man know that Vivian was not there to be picked up, but with too much alcohol hazing Big Mike's brain and his hormones rushing to all the wrong places by dancing with the luscious, tall woman, Big Mike was unwilling to back away easily. Tuck regretted that the confrontation had come to blows, but wasn't worried about a long term, negative reaction from Mike. The big man had a reputation for getting into brawls at the Tavern and seldom remembered or even cared the next day. He'd probably punch Tuck in the arm and say, "Round two tomorrow."

Tuck lengthened his stride, bone weary tired now. Emotionally exhausted, he walked with purpose toward his own home above the gift shop on Main Street. Too much thinking wasn't getting him anywhere. He didn't regret the kiss, neither one. Somehow Tuck didn't think Vivian was the fling type. She seemed more long term. The serious relationship type—something he had avoided at all costs since his marriage disaster. Yet he couldn't resist Vivian. Her facial expressions fascinated him. Pensive, compassionate, and not to mention passionate. Tuck touched his lip again. *Passionate, definitely*.

Long term and serious described his brother, Nate. Married to his high school sweetheart, two kids, a house, and car, Nate had all the fixings. Tuck had never been that way, even when he was married, no matter how short that turned out to be. Especially after that experience, he kept all relationships determinedly casual. Even his business programming style was easy. His whole motivation to make the program as easy for the end user is what had made him successful. *Goddamn Bart for blowing my business and for me for not seeing it coming.* Maybe if he was more like Nate, Tuck would have seen the writing on the wall and been able to do something about it before it all blew up in his face.

Chapter Eight

Seven would-be sailors, including Vivian, toured the vessel they would soon be manning. "It's all about the wind," Nate said when they paused by the large mast. "Without wind, no sail. The essence of sailing is the ability to read the wind, gauge the pressure of the water on the hull of the boat to propel it to the ultimate destination."

As eager as she was, learning the basics was hard work.

"No use coming on board if you don't know the terminology," Randy's graveled voice pierced the distance. "There are no *thingies* on board our ships."

Vivian was exhausted. She remembered the laugh she and Jess shared the first time they had watched a movie with their favorite comedian, and how they wondered who in the world would pay someone to be a ranch hand. "Talk about role reversal. Don't pay for the help you need, turn it into a tourist event and people will pay you to do the work," Jess said between giggles of watching the actor turn out yet another golden line.

"We sailors try to avoid the no-go-zone," Nate said, continuing his lecture on the sails. "That's when the boat comes to within forty five degrees of the wind and then the sails shake or luff, and the boat essentially stops. So that's way you see sailboats always seem to be leaning. They are actually. Sailing is a zigzag motion across the sea."

To Vivian, the terminology was the hardest, but Nate assured them that once they practiced it would come to them as easily as knowing the basics of a burger. "Port is the left side of the boat when looking forward. Compare to left, each has four letters." He smiled reassuringly. "Starboard is just like right, more letters and the opposite of left or port." Nate went on to say that the aft was the back of the boat, while astern represented the front. Vivian had always wondered about the distinction, but it suddenly made sense. Outboard, toward the edge of the boat, as in outside the hull. *Funny, I had always thought an outboard was a motor prior to today.*

"You did good, girlie," Randy said as he patted her shoulder, breaking her out of her reverie from where she stood with a half-sandwich in her hand. "Had quite a go with some of those knots, but you can climb a mast like a monkey. I was surprised."

"Why? Because, I'm female?" Vivian's tone came out more cranky than intended. She regretted her tone instantly, however, she had quite a day where her body ached in tune with her pounding head, and there just wasn't enough headache medication to cover the pounding.

Randy eyed her, taking a marginal step back. "No." He drew out the word. "Because you have never done it before."

Which was, of course, the obvious answer and made Vivian feel bad for her smart remark. She smiled in what she hoped was an apologetic manner to compensate. The smile took as much effort as everything else she did today. "I'm sorry."

"No need. Many a day I went to sea with a split head. When the trawlers use to come in here, oh, we were a rowdy bunch," he said and began to walk away. "Whiskey is you're drink is it?" He chuckled hardily.

Her hand flew to her cheek, mortified. Wasn't it bad enough that she had to live with the small snatches of embarrassing memories that assaulted her pounding head, but to find out that others knew about how she made a fool of herself, was beyond humiliation. *What was I thinking? What I did last night was both foolish and dangerous.*

Walking away, in the opposite direction, represented a better solution to her embarrassment than engaging in any conversation on the topic. Vivian made her way back to the Inn, slowly progressing toward the Mariner's Roost, while trying not to think of Tuck. She failed to stop thinking of the way his arms surrounded her, the way his lips caressed hers, and the way she had responded with abandon.

"It was the whiskey." Vivian frowned.

Even with Mike, she had been reserved. She always held back. *Why not with Tuck?* Holding back wasn't an option with him. Whenever he was around she wanted him and devil be damned the consequences. It was so unlike her typical response to men, she didn't know what to make of the situation.

As though her thoughts had conjured him, the devil himself strode her way. *Where's that crack in the Earth when I need it?* If there had been a bush or a tree to duck behind she would have done just that. The easy gait, the long stride, the life by the tail attitude that seemed to radiate from Tuck was a natural attraction for Vivian who craved that kind of let-go attitude. But she had been schooled to be cautious. Her father taught her to think and determine, assess the risks first.

Shit, Tuck saw her. Lifting his hand in salute, he walked toward her. "Hey, you." Tuck smiled.

*Oh, that smile.* So much for hiding. She longed to suffer through her pain and humiliation in private. Feeling heat rise over her face, her mind was blank of polite conversation. How could she explain last night's events? Aside from the fact she couldn't remember most of it and the snatches that she did, she would prefer to forget.

Tuck stopped directly in front of her. His silvery eyes gazed into hers as he reached out to touch her face. "Don't sweat it. It happens."

She focused on the ground, his gaze too intense to bear. "Your eye." She glanced up through the cover of her lashes at the small gash above his eyebrow and the faint, but distinguishable blue, purple, yellowing bruise along his brow bone. "I…I'm so sorry."

"I've had worse done and not even for so worthy a cause." Tuck removed his hand from her face to cup her chin, forcing her to meet his eye. Grey eyes seemed to see straight to the depths of her being.

"Really?" Vivian regretted the word as soon as it crossed her lips.

Tuck laughed. "Heading back to the Inn? I'll walk with you."

They walked in silence until Vivian stopped at the gate, her brain flooded with memories she'd prefer not to process or remember. Heated emanated from her every pore, she was sure she was aflame. Resting her hand on the gate's latch was more to sustain balance than the need to go. Desire ignited her core, leaving her at a loss at what to say or do.

Tuck covered her hand with his, pausing her retreat. "I'd like to see you again." He circled the inside of her wrist with his thumb. Her pulse jumped when his voice lowered. "You seemed to like my guitar playing. I could play for you, if you like?"

She glanced down, noticing the scuff on her otherwise white boat shoes. She swallowed. "I would." Vivian nodded. "You do play beautifully."

"Thank you." His thumb continued its sensuous massage. When his thumb hesitated, she raised her eyes to his puzzled expression. He regarded her intently, seeming to read her every thought, making her feel like an open book. "You must be tired. How about tomorrow evening?"

"I'd like that."

****

Back in her room, Vivian took deep cleansing breaths, enjoying the momentary solace. A soft knock on the door made her think Tuck had changed his mind. Maybe he wanted to spend this evening with me instead.

She opened the door a bit too eager to see the plump face of Mrs. Parson's, still flushed from the excursions of the day. "We were wondering if you would like to have dinner with your fellow sailors this evening?"

"Of course. Just let me change."

Clad in a casual, yellow sundress, Vivian made her way to the foyer to join the others.

Dinner turned out to be a lovely affair, which was comforting to her confused sensibilities and a diversion from her scrambled deliberations. She never had a one-night stand, let alone planned one out in advance, but that is exactly what she was planning for tomorrow night. There was no way she could resist Tuck and she didn't want to. She never had a fling. She was not the type of person who would hook-up with someone and then leave as though it had never happened. Had she really kissed Tuck with such complete abandon? What if he hadn't stopped? *What's come over me?* Had he wrangled her away from that big man on the dance floor?

*Just forget about it.* Toss the night up to what it was, one night of crazy. Even Marcy said Vivian tended to over-think and over-analysis everything. Everyone was entitled one night of crazy, right?

Always a lover of good stories, Vivian learned a lot of about her fellow crewmates during dinner. The pounding in her head finally gave way to the ache of her muscles.

"Well, at least you're in shape." Mrs. Parson's round face smiled. "My poor old body hasn't worked like that since the kids were small."

Putting his arm around his wife's shoulders, Mr. Parson's replied, "Nonsense." He tugged his wife close. "You're in fine shape."

Vivian marveled at their closeness. Married thirty-seven years, yet they seemed as much in love as she imagined they were when they were young. She liked to muse about happy ever after. That's why she loved the romance genre at the publishing house. The love the Parson's shared is what Vivian wanted—a marriage that was strong and lasted, a union of people who stayed together because they wanted to be together, not because they felt they should, or that it was easier to stay than to walk away. Her parents didn't seem to have what the Parson's had, at least not from Vivian's vantage point. Her parents always struck her as staying together because it took too much energy and effort to make the change.

The Jordan's were much like the Parson's, having grown closer as they got older. The Matthew's, on the other hand, were as opposite the others as a couple could get. Mrs. Matthews, Linda, had the air of superiority. She was someone who snipped and complained about everything from the size of the table to which they sat, to the state of the boat they would be soon boarding for their sailing cruise.

"I don't know." Linda complained, her thin, pinched face contorting with dissatisfaction. "The people in charge just don't seem very competent. It's certainly not what I expected."

Leaning forward on the table, Vivian rested her elbows as she picked up her tea. "What did you expect?" She tried to participate in the conversation. She had taken on the role of peacemaker of sorts, getting to know the MacLean's a bit better than the rest. Vivian felt obligated to find out the reason for the woman's displeasure and see if it could be remedied. She understood all too well that negative attitudes were infectious and if Linda continued, her attitude would infect the rest as well. "I really didn't know what to expect either, but they seem to be doing a good job with the demonstrations. We have to be safe. We paid to learn and they have an obligation to teach."

Vivian wasn't being harsh, but she did feel compelled to defend Lynette and Randy, who worked so hard. They were so warm and giving, Vivian couldn't stand for people to criticize unnecessarily.

Nodding her pumpkin orange, short curls, Clara Parson's smiled. "I agree. Arthur and I have done everything from skydiving to hitchhiking across the states and this couple, the Captain and his wife, are as nice as they come."

Having effectively shut Linda down, as people like her would only continue when she had people to feed off, Vivian asked about the many adventures the couples had shared. Howard and Janie Jordan were a relatively shy couple, studious, both accountants and resembled the part, but they smiled lots and were happy to share how every year they played tourist roulette.

Clara's eyes widened. "Tourist roulette?" Her face lit with curiosity.

"That's what we call it now. Our kids started it for us years ago. They originally called it the Holiday Wheel. The kids said we were too uptight and had to live a little." Janie reached out and tentatively touched Howard's hand. "Now we travel at the end of every tax season."

Smiling at his wife, Howard continued. "We have this wheel. The kids made it when they were youngsters and I can't see us ever throwing it away, no matter how beat up it gets."

The Jordan's had four kids who had been apparently unsatisfied with their parent's all-work-and-no-play attitude, so they made the holiday wheel, which Howard and Janie renamed, Tourist Roulette. After tax season, their kids bring out the wheel to help determine the family vacation.

Howard laughed, grabbing his wife's hand to share the cherished memory. "Remember, Janie dear, that first year when all that was on the wheel were cruises, and something else. I can't remember, but it had something to do with famous mouse."

"They wanted to go to a big amusement park like all their friends." She smiled warmly at her husband. "Terrible that they had to convince us though."

"Oh well, we got the message and they get their annual vacation." He chuckled. "Now that we're nearer retirement, we actually keep the tradition and we all go on a big family vacation once a year. Janie and I go on a separate one, just the two of us."

Watching as the couple gazed at each other, Vivian experienced an internal sigh as her heart melted. *That's what it's all about.* The love and companionship between this couple was almost palpable.

Everyone at the table exchanged stories about children, grand children, and adventures, to what they had in common and what they did for a living.

Vivian marveled how placing any group of people together in one spot for a period of time meant eventually, no matter what kind of rough start they may have, people will find common ground.

Clara and Linda flanked Vivian as they all walked back to the Inn. The men walked slightly ahead, engrossed in some sport debate over the miss of the competition runner and the conspiracy theory.

"That Nate is a looker," Clara said.

"Too bad he's married," Linda added.

"To his high school sweetheart, though." Janie smiled.

Clara squeezed Vivian's arm. "I hear Nate has a brother. A twin. Bound to be a looker too. I have only seen him from a distance. He's some sort of bookworm.

I picked that up from Ethel." She winked in response to Vivian's sidelong glance.

"He's a computer programmer," Vivian answered.

"Oh, so you met him!" Clara clapped her hands eagerly, her small body bouncing with excitement of the prospect of being a matchmaker.

"Only briefly." Vivian lied, trying to downplay the conversation and thinking of ways to change the subject. She lightly rubbed her fingers along her lips, remembering Tuck's lips on hers.

"No special someone for you, dear?" Janie asked.

"No, not now. There was someone." Vivian was content and comfortable with these women, and didn't mind sharing a bit of person information. "But it ended up he wasn't *that* special."

"Don't you worry." Linda patted Vivian's back. "The right one is just around the corner. You'll see."

The air was fresh and clean, and the company most excellent. Pleasantly tired at the evening's end, Vivian snuggled cozily into her goose down, duvet-covered bed, stretching her tired and sore muscles.

****

Randy tapped Tuck's shoulder, rounding the family dining table to set the tray of barbequed steaks and burgers in the middle. "She's a stunner, son," he said with a knowing wink, lifting a particularly large steak off the pile. "Smart too."

Tuck stared at the tray of meat, waiting for his father to lay the tongs back. Using his knife and fork, he sliced into a thick cut to see the red on the inside. His father had a habit of either over or under cooking the meat. Tuck found one, charred on the outside and blood red on the inside, just the way he likes it. He lifted the juicy piece of Alberta beef off the tray.

Nate frowned, acknowledging that Tuck was deliberately silent. "I didn't know what to expect." He placed a burger on each of the kids' plates before offering the tray to Emily. She and his mother were always the last to sit at the table. "I told Emily, prior to Vivian's arrival, that a single gal was coming to learn sailing, so we might as well put the zoo sign out and say the cougar has arrived."

Emily slapped his arm. "That's mean. I told you that then, and I tell you again in front of the family."

Nate tossed her a boyish smile, continuing. "But Dad is right, Vivian is smart. She doesn't flirt and she's not all about *look at me*. She seems very genuine on wanting to learn how to sail."

"Of course she is. What a chauvinist you are." Emily loaded her potato with sour cream and chives. "Oh, what's with you and cougars," she said between bites. "Why's it okay for men to check out women, but a single female checking out a man she's labeled as on the prowl. Tuck is single and he goes to the Tavern weekly…"

Tuck coughed, almost choking on the large forkful of steak in his mouth. He held up his hand while he took a drink of iced tea. "Hold up there." He coughed again. "I didn't say a word, so why pick on me? And I go to the Tavern to play guitar."

"Sure you do, and men go to strip clubs for the fashion show." Emily shot back.

"Not the men in this house," his mother said, standing and glancing around the table.

"Oh Ma, you know we don't." Nate laughed.

Emily held a piece of potato on the end of her fork

undeterred. "I am sure Tuck gets *lucky* at the Tavern once in a while." She nailed him with her doe-eyed gaze and smiled. "You forget what a small town we live in. People talk."

Tuck wisely refrained from commenting, so the conversation continued around him while he sat back and enjoyed the great food and family banter.

His mother cleared a few dishes from the table and brought them to the kitchen. "Well, I think Vivian is just lovely. She's well mannered, charming, and very curious about everything."

The aroma of the deep-dish, apple pie heralded his mother's re-entry. "Oh Randy, I forgot the ice cream."

"I'm on it." Tuck's father wiped the crumbs from his bushy beard with his napkin before jumping up.

Serving the slices of pie, his mother continued. "Well, I'm just saying, I liked her from the first and there'll be no more comparison to cougars where Vivian is concerned." She raised a brow at Nate, and Emily chuckled.

His father resumed his seat, scooping a generous helping of ice cream for every plate. "I agree." He bit into his pie. "Ma, you sure can cook." He swallowed his mouthful and held his fork paused above his plate. "Vivian asks lots of questions and not stupid ones either. She really wants to know how to sail." He dove his fork back into his pie. "Tucker, you're being awfully quiet this evening. It wouldn't hurt for you to get to know a nice girl like Vivian."

The door closed behind Tuck, announcing the arrival of cousin Billy.

"You adding match maker to list of services offered to clients, are ya captain?" Tuck didn't want to continue this conversation with his family. He didn't need his family's input before he had the chance to determine if they were even compatible.

"Ah, well, when lightning strikes, as they say," Randy said through another mouthful of pie.

Billy filled his plate with a burger, potato, and corn. "Fancy lot it would do him, Vivian lives on the other side of the country." The younger man added just when Tuck hoped the conversation might peter out.

Emily pushed her plate aside, having only eaten half of her pie. "I wouldn't worry about distance," she said as Nate quickly dragged her unfinished plate toward him. "When it's right, it's right. The location is here and the timing is now." She smiled at Tuck and then turned to Billy. "You get those results on your exams yet, Billy?"

As Billy launched into his discussion on school, Tuck rose from his chair. "Well, that does it for me." He took his pie with him. "When you all decide how my love life is going to turn out, you let me know."

Tuck settled on the swing on the front porch and had only taken a couple bites of the most delicious apple pie when his brother joined him.

"Sorry, man," Nate began, sitting down on the opposite side of the swing, his long legs stretched out in front of him. "Vivian is a looker though. You can't blame us for wanting someone good for you."

"You can try sucking up all you want. I am not parting with my pie." Tuck laughed.

Nate joined Tuck's laughter, moving the swing to and fro with his long legs. "It's been two years since your divorce. Isn't it time to move on?"

"Are you talking about me moving on or *getting it*

*on*," Tuck said between mouthfuls. "Let's not forget, we just met her and yet everyone assumes we're a match made in heaven."

Nate patted his knee before rising. "Tuck, man. Emily's right. You were seen at the Tavern with Vivian, and Marston has been bitching about how you were going at her in Ethel's flower garden last night…"

"We were not in the flower garden."

Nate shrugged his shoulders. "Well, wherever you were, apparently it was an intense situation, so don't sit there like this is coming out of left field, bro."

Tuck laid his empty dish to the table beside the swing. Standing from the swing, he headed across the yard to the beach. "I'm done with this conversation."

He walked along the beach toward his house. Sometimes being back home was more like taking a step back rather than moving on, and he really was trying to move on with his life. He just didn't know if Vivian was a temporary distraction.

****

The next morning dawned bright and cheery with hardly a cloud to mar the beautiful azure blue of the sky—almost white at the horizon and growing darker in hue to its apex straight above. Tuck trotted down the long set of stairs, pausing at the bottom to stretch before taking an early morning run.

He had only been called out a couple of times since re-enlisting as a reservist, and each one had a happy ending. However, after the ass-kicking he took at the pool the other day from Nate, Tuck decided he had to get back in shape. People's lives were never to be trifled with. Being a desk jockey for so long had left him soft in the haunches. He had, as his brother liked to tease, let himself go to pot.

Starting along the deserted road, admiring the sun glistening off the dew on the grass, Tuck reflected on his conversation with Nate. "You can go to the gym all you want," Nate had said. "But it's a good day's labor that will straighten you out."

The MacLean's business was multifaceted to keep them busy and afloat to use the pun year round. In the summer, they catered to tourists, and when the season moved to autumn, the family took orders for various custom-designed boats and built them over the winter. In the spring, the finished vessels would be sold to clients. Tuck had recently convinced his parents to start attending various boat shows as part of their annual planning and marketing strategy for the coming season.

Tuck continued his run, moving off the road to the trail that met the beach. While manual labor suited his father and brother, not everyone could work the way they did, or they didn't want to. Tuck loved his work and although he helped out around the warehouse, his job meant he basically sat on his ass for the majority of the day. He had an obligation to be fit for the water, so he ran most mornings outside. If the weather was too harsh, he would go to the gym, but it wasn't the same. There was nothing quite like getting up early when the gulls were just waking and the sea so calm it resembled glass where the even the tiniest ripples were visible.

Running along the trail, he remembered Vivian in his arms. He picked up his pace, imagining those long legs wrapped around him. He longed to see her expressive face suffused in passion, knowing he was the one to make her feel that way.

What bothered him most was their instant

attraction. Not even with his ex-wife had Tuck experienced such a connection. With his wife it had been a whirlwind of attending various functions, never taking the time to get to know one another before walking down the aisle. They fit naturally together that marriage just seemed like the next step. Tuck realized, too late of course, that although well suited on a social level and as long as he held a certain position, they were not suited personally. So, when the preverbal excrement hit the rotating device, she was gone as fast as she had entered his life.

Vivian seemed different and genuine. He craved to see her, but didn't want to see her again for so many reasons. In reality, he was scared of starting a serious relationship. What if he went down the wrong path with another woman not meant for him? He couldn't go through that again.

Tuck pushed his run harder. He didn't find the ideal girl right out of high school like Nate. But Vivian's slightly husky voice made him think of all things new and fresh in spring. When he closed his eyes, all he could see were those moss green eyes, almost black with passion when she kissed him. He loved the way her body moved to the music—his music, and he wanted to move with her to their own music.

"Enough," he said, checking the apparatus on his wrist for time and distance. He wiped the sweat from his brow, his body heating with wanting.

As though his thoughts had conjured her, Vivian appeared from around the corner of the Warehouse. She was moving toward him as she made her way from the road to the seaside trail. She didn't seem to spot him.

*She's singing again.* He laughed, seeing her lips move even from their relative distance.

Slowing his pace, he waited for her to notice him. His stomach flipped. *I feel like a teenager. This is crazy.*

When she finally raised those sea-foam eyes to his, he was tongue-tied.

"Hey, you," she said, stopping just a couple feet from him and pulling the ear buds from her ears. "How are you? I didn't expect to meet anyone at this hour."

"Me…either."

"Are sailors like farmers? Up with the crows?"

Tuck laughed. "I don't know many farmers, but fishermen get up early. Sailors on the other hand…"

She began to run on the spot. "Well, I won't hold you up." She turned to leave.

"How about I join you?"

In her slight hesitation, he thought he saw a mixture of shock, surprise, and fear crossed her beautiful face before she nodded. "That would be nice, but I don't run fast and you look like…" She paused, looking him up and down, her cheeks flushing in embarrassment. "You could probably out run a freight train."

"No, not a freight train. I just like to run as fast as passenger trains." He laughed.

She laughed lowering her head.

"Don't worry, I'll keep your pace."

Coiling her ear bud cord to stash it in her pocket, Vivian moved forward before stopping suddenly. "Which way?"

"What?"

"Which way? You were going one way and I the

other. Which way do you want to run?"

"Whatever way suits your fancy." He meant that statement in more ways than one.

\*\*\*\*

Vivian nodded and started to jog, Tuck at her side. *What do I talk about?* She didn't talk and jog like most people. She panted for air. Jesus, she must look a real mess soaked through and no make-up. She ran her fingers under her eyes to ensure she had no mascara streaks left over from last night.

Tuck wasn't even breathing hard. Was her heavy breathing due to her being winded or because he jogged so close beside her? She turned slightly to glance at him. His head moved to meet her gaze. He smiled a fresh-as-a-daisy smile. *Swine.* Obviously a morning man. *Uggh.*

She spotted the greenish, purple bruising along his brow bone and the small cut. Her sense of guilt renewed over the other night. Vivian stopped, bending to place her hands on her upper thighs. "Listen, Tuck." She took a moment to catch her breath, and then straightened. "I am really embarrassed about the other night. I was stupid and you were so gracious with me and getting me home safely. I am very sorry for the trouble I caused you at the Tavern."

He took a step back and his face went blank.

*Oh, shit. He's not happy.*

She wished she could read his thoughts. Finally he smiled and she released her pent up breath.

"Let's put it behind us and start fresh," he said, holding out his hand.

She slipped her hand into his, warm currents coursed up her arm at his touch. His thumb tickled her wrist, causing a soft throb in the most secret of places. Her gaze locked with his silvery, grey eyes and she was swept away on the tide of his stare.

*Ohmigod.* If he took her in his arms right now, he could have whatever he wanted, but what did Tuck want from her? Her body, her soul, just friendship, and for how long?

Chapter Nine

After another grueling day of sailing lessons, Vivian was getting ready to leave the warehouse with her team of sailors when Tuck arrived.

"Having a good time yet?"

Arthur shook Tuck's proffered hand. "What happens if we say no?"

"I'm sore as hell," Howard said.

Tuck laughed at Howard's revelation of how his father and brother worked the would-be sailors like slaves.

"Oh well, it can't be that bad." Tuck continued to shake everyone's hand, smiling easily. He returned to pat Howard on the shoulder. "As long as you're getting what you paid for." Tuck shifted a ball cap low over his forehead and combined with his sun glasses no one would see the bruising Vivian knew was there.

He went on to ask them how they found MacLean's Shipping and Restoration, whether it was from the Internet, a travel agent, or perhaps a friend. While the Matthews said their recommendation had come from a friend who did the tour last year, the rest confirmed they found the company on-line.

"Be sure to let us know if anything is not up to your satisfaction."

The room went silent and everyone glanced toward Linda Matthews, waiting for her to speak. She mellowed the last couple of days and seemed genuinely happy with the comradery of the group. Even so, Vivian was still surprised by Linda's lack of comment.

"You set sail tomorrow. We'll have a full crew on board so don't worry. The objective is to have fun. Remember, when your muscles are tired, think fun. When your eyes strain against the sun, think fun. When the Captain gets out of hand, think fun." Everyone, including Vivian, laughed hardily at Tuck's instructions. "We are here to make sure you have an adventure to relay to your kids and grand kids." Tuck nodded at Vivian. "Or to have a grand adventure."

By some unspoken general consensus, Vivian's team shuffled away leaving her alone with Tuck. He reached for her arm as she started to leave. "Are we still on for tonight? I know you leave tomorrow for the sailing cruise, but I was wondering if you would like to go out in my little sloop tonight? We could watch the sun go down?"

"That sounds like fun. Wait, Nate told us the difference between all of the different types of boats, yet you've lost me." Vivian gestured with her hand about four inches above her head. "What's a sloop?"

"Join me tonight and you'll see." Tuck smiled and winked. "Be sure to wear something warm. It can get chilly out on the water. Even in the harbor."

By the time Vivian stepped on board the small, single mast boat, her stomach was in knots of apprehension. She wanted to see Tuck again, like she hadn't wanted to see a guy since being in high school mooning over Tommy Douglas. In fact since their run that morning, she had been in a constant state of preoccupation thinking about him. *Maybe it's the way he smiles at me as if I'm the only woman in the world.* The way he spoke, with just a hint of an accent slightly different from her own, was music to her ears.

His hand warmed hers like a river through her veins as he helped her stepped from the dock onboard his sloop. "Thank you for this." Vivian said, reluctantly releasing her grip on his hand. "I didn't tell the others in case they thought I was receiving special treatment."

He squeezed her hand, not allowing her to move away. "Don't fuss about it." The warmth of his body sent tingles of electricity shooting through her arms, her legs wobbled. "They're having a good time."

"I like the way you talk." Vivian blurted, giving voice to her inner thoughts. Her cheeks grew warm.

He smiled. "People comment on the accent all the time. Car, bar, anything with an R at the end seems to bring out a drawl. It's the mix of Irish and Scott that slurred us together in to what we have now. Much like Whiskey and Ginger Ale," he added with a mischievous twinkle in his eye. "Smooth."

"I don't think I will live that down anytime soon." Vivian shook her head, laughing. She spotted his guitar close to the cabin. "What are you going to play for me tonight maestro?"

"You name it and if I can, I'll give it a whirl."

"Oh, the way you played that rock song the other night, I loved it!" Vivian gushed unashamed. She definitely wanted to listen to him play again.

\*\*\*\*

"I play better to a receptive audience." He released her hand as they settled on the deck where he had laid a comfy quilt. He had put together, what he hoped, was a romantic array of food. Some wine and cheese with a side of strawberries and red grapes sat on the edge of the blanket. Tonight, Tuck focused on seduction.

He picked up his guitar and played a tune. "I'm no Spanish guitarist."

"I wouldn't know the difference. I only know what I like."

Tuck watched her eyes smolder. *Maybe I'm not the only one focused on seduction.*

Despite the sparks or because of them, Tuck had a lot of fun. He had wanted to spend the evening with Vivian, no question about it, and he wanted to make love to her, but he didn't expect to have so much fun as well. They talked about everything from what music meant to them, to where they were when they first heard whatever song he strummed. They also chatted about their childhood and growing up, to the day he took her on his motorcycle. *Was that only a few days ago?*

Tuck loved hearing her laugh. When she was passionate about a topic, her face lit up.

"This may sound strange, but I feel more at ease with you than I have ever been with another woman."

Her cheeks turned a rosy hue, and just when he thought she wouldn't respond, she reached out to cup his cheek. "I feel the same."

Putting the guitar away, he sailed the boat out into the harbor where it drifted into a smooth rhythm. He showed her some easy things to remember when on a boat and questioned her on what she learned, allowing her to show him everything she had learned over the last couple of days. Tuck even allowed her to take the big wheel for a while. Standing back and watching her, he appreciated the sight of her body in motion. The whole evening was turning into something so much more intimate. He never expected they would get along so well, as though they had known each other for years.

She glanced over her shoulder, eyes wide with delight. "This is so much fun. It's much better than I expected."

Her cheeks were flushed when they moored the small boat. They sat back on the deck, sharing a glass of local white wine. The sun dipped into the sea when she raised her glass to his. "Cheers."

"Cheers." Tuck clinked her plastic glass with his. "Sailing can be lots of fun."

"Yes, I suppose so." Vivian nodded. "I can't imagine being a fisherman and having to do it every day, rain or shine, cold or hot."

"They do and they love it. I'm unfortunately not that kind of sailor. I am a fair weather man whereas it seems the rest of my family will go out no matter the weather and are just as content."

"With you being a rescue swimmer, bad weather would mean more to you."

"Being prepared is prepared must. Sometimes things just happen at sea that no one is prepared for. That's why they have people like me around."

"I hadn't even thought about that." Vivian sounded apprehensive. "We've had such nice weather so far. What's the forecast for the next week?"

Tuck smiled and patted her hand. "Not to worry, you will have a nice mixed bag."

"Mixed bag? What's that suppose to mean?"

"Some of this, some of that." He was deliberately vague, teasing her.

"Come on, tell me we're not going out in some

hurricane."

"Oh, wouldn't that boost business. I can see the new brochure now. Sail with us, we send you out, coming back is on you!"

Vivian laughed uproariously, grabbing her sides as tears streamed down her cheeks.

When she caught her breath, she stared at him, serious now. "No, really tell me."

"Forecast calls for a bit of a storm south and further out to sea. It's expected to keep its course East across the Atlantic and petering out there. You'll leave in sunny weather tomorrow. Then you'll hit some rain and wind from the wake of the storm, but nothing serious. The weather center keeps us informed and we will keep the team updated."

"But I can hardly get a single bar here on my phone. What will it be like when we leave shore?" Vivian eyes shone with innocence.

Tuck laughed and shook his head. "Might as well save your battery. It's not likely to get a signal. There are no cell towers at sea. The ship comes equipped with satellite phone and all other communication essentials. We don't expect our sailors to be texting while at sea."

She tilted her head back and he followed her gaze. The darkening sky twinkled with stars. "Look, Tuck." Vivian pointed. "I know you get to see this all the time, but I don't think I've ever seen a sky so alive. Even where I live in the country, the sky is beautiful, but this is different and you have it all the time."

Tuck pulled her down on the blanket he had spread for their dinner. He lay by her side, gazing at the stars. "It's funny when you live here and seem to take it for granted."

"I know." She peered out to the distant horizon. "There are lots of things I take for granted too."

"Like what?"

"Like my friends, and how lucky I am to have a job that's flexible enough to allow me to run the café even if it only breaks a small profit. Marcy and I do it because we love it. We don't need to be big business owners, but I'm lucky. Most people don't get a choice."

"I know what you mean." Tuck did know what she meant, having witnessed so many fishing families go under over the years and have to move away for work. He had seen the small town where he and Nate grew up, reduced to almost a ghost town before the Town Council and a few of the more influential residents decided to make their mark on the map and become a tourist community. People didn't like the change, but change was keeping this town from disappearing.

Resting on his elbows, he turned to her. "Even for me, I was lucky to have a fall-back position when the Tech Bubble burst. Sometimes it's easy to feel sorry for my loss, but hey, I am lucky. How many people went under and were never able to resurface because they didn't have the same opportunities I had."

"So we're a couple of lucky ducks then." She grinned. The warmth of her breath fanned his face over the couple of inches that separated them.

Whether he moved or she moved or they both did, he didn't know, and he didn't care because when their lips touched it was magic—tender with a large dose of instant passion.

****

Vivian's lips parted to allow Tuck access, and he marched right in like he owned the place. Their mutual

133

desire quickly intensified their carnal hunger for each other. Her fingers played with the lobe of his ear, while his hand caressed her hip. His other hand sought the back of her neck and pulled her close so she was locked in his embrace. He released her neck to caress her cheek.

"You're so beautiful," he murmured against her lips. Vivian's heart drifted, lost in a tidal wave of glorious emotions. Tuck made her feel beautiful. She didn't feel gangly or awkward around him. They fit naturally.

Tuck moved and suddenly she was under him, his weight on his elbows as he deepened the kiss. The electrifying passion soared as he nipped her lip, along her jaw, and to the very sensitive area below her ear.

Vivian sighed, tipping her head back. "That feels so good."

Tuck lifted his head to stare deeply into her eyes, leaving her beret without his lips on her own. His eyes were darkened by desire that leapt to the surface. He was the spark that would make her burn with fiery embers.

"W...we, ah, we...should," Tuck stammered, seeming at a loss of how to phrase his words. "I don't normally do this. I don't want you to get the wrong idea."

Vivian's fingers moved from his hair to his lips, shushing his words. She understood, he was concerned about stopping what they were starting. "I don't do this either...ever, but tonight no talking. Tuck, you're what I need, right now. You're who I want."

And he was perfect.

Watching the turn of emotions and pleasure cross

his face, Vivian felt unaccountably in control. Wanton even as she undid the buttons of his shirt. She wanted him and she didn't want him to doubt just how much. She slid her fingers inside his shirt to splay them along his muscular pecks, lightly tracing her fingers down his abdomen. He was sprinkled with a fine film of hair that matted over his nipples, joining to run down a line to his center hardness.

Tuck pulled her sweater over her head, then her long sleeved T-shirt, followed by a strappy camisole. When he reached her bra, he heaved a sigh. "Whew, I thought I'd never get through the layers."

Only Tuck could pull off easy banter in the mist of passion, causing Vivian to giggle like a little girl. "Well, you did say to dress warm."

"What was I thinking?" He bent to nibble the bared flesh above her lacy bra. "What was I thinking?"

"Stop thinking." Vivian ran her fingers through his short, military-style hair. She arched her back, pushing her breasts closer to him, the heat in her own core making her determined and bold. A throb assaulted her lower limbs, licking its flames throughout her body. Wherever Tuck touched, she burned for more.

With a flick of his practiced hand, her breasts were freed from the confines of her bra. He ran his hands down her length, pausing to gaze at her as though he were savoring a buffet. She stared back, watching as he bent to lightly flick his tongue over her rosy buds. While his teeth nipped one erect nipple, his hand squeezed the other. Her hand cupped his, encouraging him.

"Take it in your mouth." Her breath escaped her as she arched forward.

\*\*\*\*

Tuck's craving went wild for her. Never had he been with a woman who would tell him what she wanted. She threw her head back and her hands moved into his hair as her hips thrust to grind into him in the same rhythmic motion as the boat rocking gently on the waves. He wanted her now, but was enjoying the moment. As each passionate wave strung together, he wanted it to last, and didn't want to rush their first night together.

Her eyes were luminous in the near darkness, reflecting the string of fairy lights that ran down the mast. Her hands moved from his hair, down the sides of his body, to his pants, undoing the buckle and zipper and sliding them off his narrow hips. Not to be outdone, Tuck encircled her hips and her jeans quickly followed his.

Clad only in gauzy panties and he sat back on his haunches to admire the vision. He savored the length of her spread like dinner on the patched quilt. Magnificence highlighted her fine lines. Her left knee raised slightly as her breast heaved. She stared at him as though he was her next meal and he was happy to comply. *She looks rather tasty herself.* Slowly removing her panties, he laid beside her. She took his manhood in her hands, running her thumb over the sensitive skin at the head, while her fingers increased and decreased pressure, running up and down its smooth length.

Tuck ran his hand over her abdomen, to the cleft between her thighs, gently nipping the sensitive skin between her legs. Her hands moved from him to cup her own breasts. She gazed at him intently, as if challenging him to continue. Her fingers skimmed her own body, sliding over her hips as she parted her legs, drawing herself open and allowing him full access.

As his tongue flicked and his fingers massaged the outside lips, her husky voice moaned his name. "Oh yes, Tuck."

She raised her hips as he drank from her nectar. The vibrations of her shutter confirmed her heightened arousal. He nipped the inside of her thigh and continued across her abdomen, kissing and savoring ever inch until his lips embraced hers again. She tangled her hands in his hair, pulling him close. Her tongue dueled with his in the age-old combat of desire. His hand retraced the path down her body while her hand encircled his pulsating manhood.

He slipped his fingers inside her moist opening to the spongy inside pulsating with wanting. She cried out. "Ahhh."

"Yes," he said, submerged in the hunger her response ignited in him. The more responsive she was, the more enflamed he became. He could barely hold back as her lips moved down his body, taking his nipple between her teeth. It was his turn to pant when she took his length inside her mouth, sucking gently, swirling her tongue over the tip. "Ohmigod, Vivian. I can't hold on."

She glanced up and smiled like the cat with the canary, moving slowly over his abdomen until she claimed his lips.

Not to be outdone, he placed one hand behind her head and the other at the small of her back as he flipped her onto her back, running his hands down her sides. Vivian spread her hands across the blanket in welcoming. He knelt between her legs, holding her hips as he slipped into her depths.

From the first thrust it was an explosion of color and sensation unlike anything else. The water lapped against the side of the boat, rocking them. As one, they rocked in rhythm, glimmering with sweat their joint need sedated. Her passion pulsed around his shaft, drawing him home. She pulled him to her, wrapping her legs around him as they moved as one. He was building fast, losing control. He stared at her as she shattered around him, finally let go.

Tuck kissed her as she came back to reality, his mouth gentle on hers. Her gaze was like water running over moss in a small spring—clear and liquid. His own body, languid locked within hers in a fluidity of connection, was a new sensation for him. He didn't want to think about this ever coming to an end. He just wanted to focus on the here and now.

Kissing her eyelids as they fluttered. "Welcome back." He tenderly kissed her forehead, moving slightly so she rested in the crook of his arm. He pulled the edge of the blanket up to cover them as they lay in harmonic silence, watching the stars and enjoying the sensation of the gentle sway of the boat lulling them to sleep.

****

Tonight represented an entirely new experience. In no previous encounter had Vivian ever taken the lead as she had with Tuck. She had also never experience such an orgasm. Reveling in the wanton sensation, she delighted in the power it provided. She didn't know what had come over her, but she had no remorse. With Mark she had been timid when they made love and she wasn't as fulfilled as she felt right now. With Tuck

138

everything was different. He was so natural and real, like she had already known him forever instead of a few days. She was herself with him. She wanted Tucker MacLean in her life, long term.

The sky changed from indigo to black as night descended over them, and the stars brightened with intensity. Vivian lay against Tuck, enjoying his warmth, and running her hands lightly over his chest. Words weren't spoken, they weren't necessary. This moment was beyond words.

His body shifted and he hardened against her, smiling. She turned and as his muscles tensed ever so slightly. Vivian mounted him, triumphant as he filled her. Lifting up and lowering down, she watched hunger fill his eyes. She bent to nip his neck and took his nipples in her mouth. She was in total control. When his hands cupped her breasts, she tilted her head back and gave into the pleasure he provided.

Rocking, moving, swaying, and gripping, she rode him like a stallion until his body tensed and convulsed, joining her release. "Yes." Her breathy whisper crossed her kiss-swollen lips. *This* is what she wanted.

****

In early dawn, Tuck walked her back to the Inn. Holding her hand and content in her company, he watched the sky descend from darkness as the stars yawned out of sight. Though he hadn't slept much, he wasn't tired. Tuck could run a marathon.

He opened his mouth to tell her how much he had enjoyed their night together, and how much she had come to mean to him, but she shushed him with a finger over his lips.

"It is what it is," Vivian said in her husky tone. "It

139

was beautiful and I have no regrets. What about you?"

He dipped his head to kiss her lips in a gentle caress. "None," he said, moving to hold possession of her mouth one more time, his tongue finding hers. His own voice filled with renewed desire as he paused to stare deep into her eyes. "I want to see you again."

Her eyes were dazed with yearning. Vivian nodded before turning to walk inside the Inn. He held her hand, clasped in his own, one final second. Tuck brought their clasped hands to his lips, gently kissing the inside of her wrist.

When the door closed behind Vivian, Tuck feared he would never again be able to capture the depth of emotional connection he shared with Vivian last night. For the first time in his life he was optimistic that every night with her would be a new discovery.

Chapter Ten

Lynette, Tuck, Agnes, and Ethel all lined the hill leading to the open water as the tall ship set sail. The ship sported three beautiful masts, each with its sail fully furled. With everyone in their designated position, for those in love with the sea, the departure was a sight that never got tired. Randy took them into the harbor until they entered the open water, passing their farewell committee.

Randy checked the compass, and tapped his finger on various gadgets. He stood straight at the helm and saluted his wife as they passed. "A traditional sailor would frown, preferring wind power the whole voyage." His strong hands wrapped around the wheel. "A smart sailor knows when to tact to the wind and when to use the motor to avoid perilous situations."

Vivian leaned on the rail and lifted her hand in salute, gazing at Tuck from the growing distance. Her eyes widened when he laid his hand over his heart before waving good-bye. She blinked. *Did I just see that or was that some trick of the sun on the water?* Her own hand went to her chest.

They entered open water, and Tuck was now a speck in the distance. Randy called for his new sailors to take their positions. For the first while, a few of the team had trouble keeping their balance on deck, but by the end of the first day, they were all seasoned as they gained their sea legs. At least the *real* crew made the trainees feel confident. Truth be told, they were a nervous lot eager to prove their abilities. Randy and Nate had done their job well in getting everyone prepared. Vivian felt their first day was a success.

Clear skies and fair winds took the ship to the open sea so that by nightfall, even through the looking glass, land was now a memory. Sea birds no longer circled.

Vivian could read about this experience all she wanted, however, nothing would have prepared her for the complete and utter freedom the sea provided. The work was hard for someone who was not accustomed to the range of motion, but everyone continued to be encouraging. Howard seemed fascinated by navigating by the sky and stars, and who would have thought someone like Linda would enjoy rope tying. Vivian loved climbing the masts to tend to the sheets, otherwise known as the sails.

Making her way up the steep mast to the crow's nest, suspended above the moving ocean and the wind whistling its tune as they zigged and zagged, tacking to the wind, Vivian thought she was truly flying. She could not imagine anything making her feel this exhilaration with a distinct sense of danger hovering on the edge. Sometimes the ship tilted so that one false step, she knew she would be overboard.

Nate waited by the mast as she slowly climbed down. "Oh, I think, you've got the bug," he said compatibly.

"I think maybe." Vivian agreed, nodding ascent. "I keep saying it, but it's true. I just didn't know what I was signing up for when I contacted you. I wanted a sense of adventure, but this is something…"

"Something else, I know. We grew up with the sea. Salt water runs in our veins, but every once and a while we see someone who come to the sea unexpectedly and you know what?" Nate spoke louder to be heard above the rising wind as they made their way to the mess for another of cook's fabulous dinners. "They come back. And I suspect you will as well."

"I wouldn't mind."

By the end of the second day, Vivian remembered Tuck's weather forecast and was not concerned by the whistling wind or the overcast sky. "Tuck said we may get some unsettled weather," she said, standing by Randy in the wheelhouse.

"Did he now?"

Vivian stared through the large window at the purple hued horizon, refusing to give anything away. If Tuck wanted his family to know about them, it was up to him to tell them. "Yes. I'm certainly glad I purchased this wooly sweater in town before we left."

Randy snorted. "What'd they charge for that?"

Vivian inspected her heavy corded, beige sweater under her bright yellow slicker. She smiled. "Doesn't matter, I'm warm and dry."

"That's the main thing." He checked the ship's instruments. "My Ma use to knit those types of sweaters for all us kids. Scandalous what they charge for them now."

"Well, we tourists expect to pay a little more for some things."

"As long as you feel it was worth it."

"On a day like today…" She paused, gazing at the deck being sprayed by the salty ocean current. "For sure."

Nate came up from below deck. "Bit of weather coming our way," he said. "Ma says tropical storm in the gulf, but we should be able to stay out of its path. It's headed farther out to sea so we're gonna catch the tail as it heads away. Everyone okay with that?"

"Our mast monkey here already had the storm gist from Tuck." Randy pointed a thumb in Vivian's direction. "It's okay though. She's dressed to keep the chill from the blowing water off the bone." He teased, gently shoving an elbow to her ribs.

"Tuck said not to be concerned, that it would breeze by us." At Nate's intense stare, Vivian continued with uncertainty. "He just said that this is what it is to be expected where everything is dependent on wind and weather. He reassured me the crew, being so excellent and all, would take care of us, and that you were all use to this kind of thing."

Nate turned to his father, eyebrow raised. "Said all that did he?"

"Was he wrong to say anything?"

"Ah, no." Randy said and shook his head, a smile on his thin lips. "Just surprises us. We didn't know you had spent so much time with Tuck."

*Oh, shit. I said too much.* Vivian started to back out of the wheelhouse.

Nate held up a hand. "Hey, now. You don't have to leave."

"Ah, it's okay. I promised the ladies I'd play a game a crib with them this evening."

****

Tuck monitored the weather on three large flat screens attached to the wall where he worked. "I don't like the look of this, Ma." Tuck pointed to one of the computer screens. "Look here." He tapped the screen over a red swirl. "That tropical storm from the south has taken a sharp turn and is heading back in, and there, see the current." He pointed to another screen where long blue lines filled the monitor. "That's the cold air coming from the North, colliding with the warm Gulf Stream heading up to meet it."

Tuck turned his head from the monitors to glance at his mother. She stared at the computer screen, shaking her head.

"You see here, that's the tropical storm everyone focused on and rightly so. We had the Navigator change the course to avoid the brunt. They'd only feel the licks of the tail. All the reports said the storm would head further out to sea and peter out in the cold water." Tuck illustrated by pointing to another spot on his digital map. "But if you check this warm Gulf Stream motion here, if the storm stays in its present course, after the hair-pin turn it took, you know what happens when warm meets the cold—they collide."

His mother nodded. "I'll radio the Navigator and let them know. Can you send them a picture of this?" His mother waved her hands at the mass of screens. "Tuck?"

"I'm doing it now," he confirmed.

Tuck had a bad premonition swimming in the pit of his belly. He couldn't shake it. The rain started about noon on the second day of the voyage. His father had sent through reports that although the wind was up, they hadn't received the rain by that point. Tuck continued to watch the weather patterns and compared them to the log the Navigator had filed. No matter how he made adjustments and communicated back and forth to the

Navigator, he just didn't see how they were going to avoid some very rough sea. *Goddamnit, I told Vivian all would be fine.*

Heading back toward land at this point was not an option as that is where the majority of the activity of the storm lay, close along the coastal line. The crew was better off out to sea at this point by all estimations. However, with the gulf current changing he didn't see where the ship could chart to avoid one or the other of the storms, and be lucky enough to avoid the inevitable collision of both. Growing up by the ocean, if there was one thing Tuck had learned about Mother Nature was that she loved a good fight and the collision of these two weather systems was going to be a doozy.

Focusing on his monitor, hoping to force the weather to do what he wanted, he remembered his words to Vivian. *I'm a fair weather sailor.* He hadn't lied. He hated the wind and driving rain, but what he didn't tell her was the reason he was a fair weather sailor—he would be called out on the chopper to jump into the sea to rescue the all-weather sailors at risk in storms just like this. He didn't want to scare her.

Tuck would trade places with Vivian in a heartbeat to ensure her safety through this oncoming beast. Closing his eyes, he imagined the sway of the ship under his feet, envisioning Vivian walking, struggling for proper footing on the rain soaked oak deck. His father and brother were exceptional sailors, and Tuck had no fear of their sailing ability, but when Mother Nature decided to show her wrath, no man or beast would stand in her way.

Tuck scrutinized the charts. "Heaven help them."

\*\*\*\*

The crew, both seasoned and beginner, had been working in shifts, adjusting ropes, checking the sails, and keeping up with the multitude of duties required on a ship as large as the Navigator. Captain MacLean, Randy's name at sea, put a halt to commotion and gathered the tourists inside the wheelhouse.

Running his weathered hand down his face to wipe the moisture from his beard, Randy began. "I'm no good at mincing words, so I won't." His graveled voice was more hoarse than usual. He paused, blinking the rain out of his eyes "The latest weather charts show that we've had a collision of sorts out here. A high and low collided, a warm and cold. The result will be bad. I've already informed my crew and they are preparing. There's nothing else to be done but ride it out."

Vivian watched the women's faces fill with fear as they gravitated to their men. She had no one, so she simply stared ahead straight into the depths of Randy's deep brown eyes. Her eyes probably resembled a doe's eyes, caught in a bright light. Randy had no control over the weather. He could only control the ship holding them within the mighty force.

Clara linked her hand in Arthur's. "Y…you've been through a storm like this before though, right?"

Nate stepped beside his father. "Of course, but you haven't and as we told you from the beginning, it is always best to be prepared."

The captain nodded. "We watch the weather like a beacon. That's our job. This is a complete fluke phenomenon out here now. Something Poseidon likes to spring on us once in a while just to let us know he's still in charge." His tone sounded resolute. "We would never have begun the voyage had we known of the two storms. The one on radar was expected to head out to sea, but she took a turn for the worse. She's now heading back toward the coast just as the cold water from the North is coming down, colliding with the warm Gulf Stream."

"What does this mean?" Linda's voice was higher pitched than normal. "Can't we just go back? Surely we can't be that far out to sea that we can't go back."

Nate shook his head. "No, we're not that far out, but returning is not an option." He pulled up the weather radar and the men stepped closer. "The worst of it appears to be the tropical storm. She's hugging the shoreline, so we don't want to go through that. The hurricane is causing the cold current to move inland, effectively trapping us from going ashore."

"It's best for us to continue to head further out to sea," said Captain MacLean.

"What about running parallel to the storm?" said the ever-practical Howard, adjusting his glasses. He resembled what Vivian imagined an accountant to look like. She could almost envision numbers crunching in his head.

Nate nodded. "That's good thinking, there, Howard." He turned to the charts on the table. "And that is effectively what we have been doing the last twelve hours, but it looks as though the mouth of the pincers have closed the gap we were running for. Now we have to run through the collision of the two storms in order to get out of it. We definitely don't want to keep running with it."

Everyone's face mirrored Vivian's stare of horror. Captain MacLean held up his hand. "We've been through this before and we'll get through it again. We'll be okay. We just want to make sure you understand what's going on. We'll face this bastard storm and we'll get through it. You'll be surprised when we come out the other side. The sky will be so clear, you'll swear you can reach up and touch the face of God. And what a story you'll have to tell!" His smile was forced even as he winked.

"Make sure you have your life jackets on." Nate pointed to the supply bunks by the door as they parted.

Collectively, the small group donned their life jackets under their rain slickers and set about their assigned chores. There was no shift work now, all hands on deck. Better to be busy anyway. Sitting around thinking about the storm would only make it worse.

"Okay, monkey woman." Captain MacLean laughed, smiling at Vivian. "You go with Gabriel and climb up and take down those sails. We've no need of a foul wind pulling us under. We'll go with the engine in this mess."

Vivian had never been one to be scared of heights, which is why she loved her assigned job of unfurling the sails, but now what had appeared to be a tall ship in port was suddenly small in this great big ocean. She grew more petrified with each step as she fit her feet to the small rungs on the mast. The ship listed this way and that as she climbed higher. At times she seemed to be hanging in mid air over the berth of the sea as it waited to swallow her. The rubber soles of her shoes slipped and her knees squeezed tight around the mast, her hands, white knuckled, held firm to the handholds. She no longer reveled in the free sensation of flying of just yesterday. With the imposing danger of the storm and the roll of the ship, at times she was almost paralyzed to move her muscles and get the job done. Her shoulders ached and she thought her hands would never keep their grip, but she marveled the strength from her body. *I have to keep going, people are depending on me.* So she kept going.

The hours went on and on. The sea continued to rage and get angrier still. Vivian had seen movies that depicted high waves, but they were full of shit compared to the real thing. She zigzagged across the slick decking, trying to keep her feet from failing her.

She never understood the feeling of cold terror running through her veins until she saw a twenty-five-foot wave crashing down with the next one waiting. The sheer weight of the water bearing down on the ship caused vibrations from the timbers to course up her legs.

Captain MacLean insisted that anyone on deck be tied. "It's an ancient course of action, but to this day the most effective means of keeping people on board a vessel in a storm like this." He shouted over the ranging wind as he lashed the ropes.

Howling wails from a medieval novel is the best description of the wind. Within a few hours of the storm gaining force, two of the three ladies, Janie and Linda, were so scared they were beyond providing any help. Clara, a kindly heart by nature, accompanied the women below to take care of them, ensuring the rest of the crew could concentrate. Arthur, amazingly enough, was as solid as a rock, doing what he was told, when he told, the fear in his eyes never halting his motions. Howard seemed to come into his own, removing his glasses every once and while to wipe them on his sleeve, he was in the thick of the action, moving like he'd been born to it. Born to it or not, by early the next morning, after a couple hours of rest, the crew, seasoned or no, were exhausted.

*When will we come out the other side? It's been so long.* Vivian's shoulders were knotted. She reached a hand under her woolen sweater to the cotton shirt to massage the ache. They were fighting waves that seem to be increasing in size for more than a day. Vivian didn't want to ask, for she didn't want to appear weak, but this went a little bit beyond the adventure she signed up for. *This must be a dream gone bad.* She pinched her shoulder, a weak attempt to wake up.

Howard approached as she sipped her coffee, warming her hands around the large mug. He forced a smiled, seeming to read her her fear, which she was sure passed very clearly across her face. Everyone struggled to keep food and liquid down as the ship listed from one side to the next. Standing, Vivian hoped the scalding liquid would not run over her fingers as she moved her weight from her left foot to her right and back again in motion with the ship. "I can't sit down. I'm too antsy."

Howard removed his glasses, wiping his spectacles with his hanky. "Amazing," he said, a twinkle of excitement glowed in his deep-set brown eyes. "To think we're only hitting the collision of the two storms now. It will be rough for the next few hours. The captain thinks we'll be out of the worse of it by nightfall tomorrow, and if we're able to keep the course, we should be clear by the next day."

"What?" Vivian almost choked on her coffee. "You can't be serious? What? We have to go through another day of this? What have we been going through so far if this isn't *the storm*?"

Howard raised a hand in a peace offering, and hitched his glasses back around his ears. "That was the tropical storm that turned back toward the land, but there is a hurricane now to contend with from the south." He adjusted his glasses, giving her a sympathetic smile. "Perhaps you want to join the other ladies."

She shook her head. "Like hell," Vivian said instantly, aiming for some bravado she certainly didn't feel. When they made it through this, she wanted Tuck to know she had been brawn and strong. She didn't want to walk away and think back about what she should have done. She wanted to be a part of it. "Captain Maclean says it'll be a hell of a story to tell. I'm not missing the fun. Not on your life."

"That's a girl." Howard smiled and left her to go check on his wife. "Captain MacLean's presently running a course through the troughs of the waves, but at some point he has to turn the ship into the waves. When he does, he says we'll have to brace ourselves for that will be the worst part."

Vivian couldn't believe what she was seeing when she went back on deck. Waves, seemingly as large as buildings, writhed on either side of the ship. She cringed at the thought of having to puncture the depths of one of those monsters to get through the storm. Passing over those waves seemed impossible. They were imposing rock walls, and the ship was a toothpick floating in a bathtub, waiting for a child to send it down the drain.

Nate moved toward her, his gait unsteady. "There

she is." He shouted to be heard. "You doing okay?"

Vivian nodded, sure her eyes were as big as saucers. Her fear of the waves and what she would face when she stepped over the threshold was holding her rooted to the spot. Words were beyond her for the moment.

Nate's eyes, so much like his brothers, their color mirroring the consistency of the ranging ocean on either side, stared at her with concern.

"I'm fine," Vivian said, finding her voice. "What can I do?"

Nate squeezed her shoulder and told her what was required. "Everything gets braced for the next assault. Double-check all the hatches. We check everything twice. Tie it down, tie it up, make sure it's secure and don't forget to tie yourself. The captain is watching the movement to time our transition through the wave from the trough we have been enjoying."

"Oh…okay." Vivian managed find her voice.

Connecting her harness, Vivian, along with others went about their jobs, sloshing, falling, listing, and generally trying to maintain footing. She was so cold, chilled to the very bone that she wasn't sure if she would ever be warm again. She experimentally wiggled her toes in her new boat shoes, which didn't look new anymore, just to know they were still working. She wondered how she ever could have been concerned with her planned outfit. *Look at me now. Clothes ruined and I'm scared out of my mind that I'm not going to make it back to shore.* Vivian tried to think of a really scary roller coaster ride—thrilled and scared for your life, but always came out the other side. *Maybe if I close my eyes tight the ride would be over.*

Chapter Eleven

Vivian finished her checklist and returned to the wheelhouse to see yet another monstrous wave crash on the deck and flow over their heads. How much could this ship take before it succumbed to the weight of the water bearing it down? What would happen if the wood splintered? The logical side of her brain kicked in, and she remembered the safety drills. She was confident she would know what to do *if* it came to that. But if she was this scared on such a large vessel, what would it be like out on the open water with the gigantic waves bearing down on a lifeboat? In her present state of mind, it gave her no comfort to think about the what-ifs.

She did think about her mom, dad, and brothers. Her nephews would take good care of Snickerdoodle. *Stop-it!* She admonished the thought even as she pictured the faces of her nephews and two godchildren, Marcy's kids. Closing her eyes, Vivian could hear their giggles. Tuck and his mesmerizing, silver eyes entered her thoughts. Her breathing deepened. Everything else faded like the flashes of lighting. Visions of Tuck remained in her mind's focus and ironically the image of him calmed her.

Vivian was brought up short from her reverie by Randy's authority voice. "We're here," he announced. "This is where the devil does his battle!"

Vivian shivered. That didn't sound like a good

place to be at all!

In a mere second, the situation went from bad to worse. Now mixed with driving rain, flashes of lightning and reverberating boom of thunder filled the sky. The howling wind picked up, and the vessel was tossed about as a child would hurl their soap during a bath. Unable to hold anything in her shaky hands, Vivian tucked the bottle of water in the side pocket of her yellow slicker.

Lightning flashed again and the boom of thunder soon followed. *So much for counting Mississippi's to gauge the distance from the storm.* Flash with an instant crash surrounded the ship. Small bits of hail assaulted her along with the pelting rain. Holding tight to the railing, her feet were spread wide to accommodate the swaying of the ship.

Hearing a loud crack, Vivian quickly turned.

Nate, the only one still out on deck, was sent to re-tie the canvas that had started to billow as a knot loosened in the driving wind and rain.

She reacted without thinking. Moving like a drunk on a late Saturday night, Vivian grabbed Captain MacLean's arm. "It's coming down!" She shouted as loud as she could to get his attention.

He turned his head to glance at her before focusing back on his task. "What?"

*It's no use. He can't do anything. He's needed at the wheel.*

Shouts of one sort or another were being bellowed. She left the captain and rushed to the door. She wrenched open the wheelhouse door and sloshed onto the deck, trying desperately to keep her footing, her drive to warn Nate propelling her.

Holding onto the railing to retain her footing, her shout was nothing more than a puff of air lost in the wind. "The mast! The mast is coming down!" She pointed at the weakening post.

A blinding blue-silver ball travelled down the pole and across the planks to bounce close to her feet as she struggled forward—almost bent to get through the pressure of the wind and pelting rain. *St. Elmo's Fire!* Vivian had read about this phenomenon and knew enough to keep her distance, but that was easier said than done in present circumstances. *St. Elmo's Fire* was lightning seeking a home to explode upon, frying everything in its wake.

Nate was exposed and she had to get to him. She reached for Nate's towline as the ball scooted up the mast. Vivian was out of time. With all her strength, she pulled the line. Nate finally turned to her. He shouted something she couldn't hear. She pointed to the climbing ball of fire and wrenched his rope again, waving one of her hands to motion him toward her and out of danger.

The wood splintered and once the ball exploded that mast would come down. She *had* to get Nate out of the path of the lightning ball and impending doom. When the mast fell, it would fall like an ancient oak in the forest, crashing everything in its path. She couldn't let Tuck's brother be in that pathway.

Nate slipped and slid toward her just as the Navigator plowed the crest of a wave. The captain would be unable to change course of the vessel despite what may be going on at this point.

Vivian stared as a spectacular accumulation of catastrophic events unfolded before her very eyes as though scripted in a movie scene. She pointed to the crack in the mast again. "It's coming down! Get out of the way!"

Like fireworks in the air, the fireball exploded off the end of the pole. Pull as she might, Nate remained directly in the path of the falling mast and the wall water coming over the side. How in the world did she ever think this vessel was large? Surely to God that wave must be fifty-feet high and this ship not big enough to take that kind of hit.

Nate regained his footing only to fall again as Vivian retained hold of his line and the railing. She and Nate glanced up at the firework display, not one bit diminished by the water pour down. The post groaned loose on its end, moving with the motion of the boat. Then it started to topple in slow motion. Nate hadn't cleared the path. Nate, with the same eyes as Tuck's, would be a goner. Vivian must get him out of the way or that fate would be a certainty.

With strength she did not know she possessed, Vivian let go of the railing and with the line held tightly in both hands, heaved with all her might. Nate once again found his feet, both hands reaching for the life saving cable that slid and skidded across the deck toward her. Then the wave crashed down, taking the mast and them with it.

Nate was safely out of the path of the mast, but Vivian was lifted by the water, her feet no longer in contact with the ship. Nate flailed to reach her hands, managing to grab hold of one her wrists just as they were tossed off the side of the boat and into the ranging sea. One hideous wave replaced another crashing down in its place. Together, with a tangle of splintered wood, ropes, and rigging, they were flung free of the boat and into the boiling mass of cold, open ocean.

A wave, with the force of a swinging baseball bat, smashed into Vivian's forehead. She saw stars and gulped for precious air, unable to distinguish between up or down. Grateful for the firm hold of Nate's hand on her own, her other arm flailed in the roiling water as she tried to find the surface. *I can't catch my breath. There is no surface.*

She heard shouts, but couldn't place the direction. He ears filled with the gargle of the sea. Darkness with flashes of light filled her vision. In between the sparks, she saw Nate struggling as well.

Something was tangled around her leg. Vivian saw the coiling rope fixed to her ankle. The cable tightened with each kick of her foot as she tried to get unsnarled. She should stop kicking, but her need for air and the confusion over which way was up, only served to further ensnare her in the lines.

"Uggkk." Bubbled from her lips as the dropping weight of the mast pulled her down into the cold, deep unknown. Panicked, she lifted her leg into a crouch to free the snare, but the wet cord wouldn't unleash its grip. With each effort to tug her leg free, the rope tightened, digging more severely into her skin. *I'm not ready to go!* She frantically reached for Nate's arm, but she couldn't get hold as she continued to fall, spread eagle, dragging him along with her.

Then, like a buoy, her life jacket popped, springing her up out of the water. She gasped for the life giving air before the deep sea yanked her under again. *We are going down.* She was frantic surrounded in the blue-grey swirling water. An eerie calm descended as she broke to the surface again. She gulped all the air she could into her lungs and forced her mind to work. The first rule she had learned in her Bronze Cross swimming training was to stay calm when others were not. *Better said than done at this point.* Quivering as she might be on the inside, Vivian forced her flailing arms to relax.

Nate's hand was like a death grip on her wrist. They made eye contact briefly before the next thousand pounds of water sent them under. She just barely saw the disappearing length of splintered timber, lines, and rigging fanning out like hair on a doll, the canvas having unrolled and floating free like a giant cape.

The tugging on her ankle increased. She was running out of time. Survival meant getting out of the snarl of ropes or she would never be able to buoy back up. Nate was tied to the boat by his harness, but she had run out of the wheelhouse so fast with only one thing on her mind, saving Nate. She hadn't attached her harness. If she didn't get free, they were both going down—fast.

Timing as much as she could, when next they surfaced she pulled on Nate's hand. "I'm caught up in the rigging. I have to get my leg free or we're going down!"

He nodded. "I've got my knife!" Nate shouted just before they were under again.

In his free hand he gripped a knife, but she couldn't reach it, the the pull downward exhausting her slithering energy. *I'm out of time.* As tight as his hold was, he couldn't drag the weight attached to her leg. Nate's hand slipped on her wrist. *He can't hold me!*

It happened too fast. She saw the flash of metal

catch on the lights from above the waterline and with a last ditch effort Nate flung the blade through the water in her direction. Reaching with the tips of her fingers, she missed and Nate's grip was lost. Vivian was tugged downward out of his reach.

She reached for him, but the distance swelled. His life jacket pulled him to the surface as she went further down. The last thing she heard was him shouting *no!*

****

Tuck was monitoring boat traffic on the old fashioned CB radio tuned for boat traffic. His worse fear was realized when he upped the volume, his father's voice relaying the first SOS.

"Vessel in distress. Coordinates provided."

Tuck swore his heart stopped, having never imagined any vessel under his father's command would dare to be in distress.

Then the next SOS. "All available vessels within range to come to aid of sailing school tall ship taking on water. Two souls overboard. Coordinates provided. Repeat, two overboard."

Tuck held his breath as another SOS came through. "All available hands are on deck. One life rescued from water. Another still missing. Storm not letting up. Vessel in distress. Coordinates provided. One life saved. One soul still missing at sea. Rescue attempt failed."

With a hand over his eyes, Tuck couldn't believe what he had heard. The hand held radio lay on the table in front of him as though diseased. The landline cradled in his other hand, Coast Guard on the phone. "There was no way a storm like this was not properly forecast. What have we sent those people into? The storm

160

changed its path so rapidly and without time to prepare."

Tuck had already received a call from the reserves to activate into service when the distress signal came in from the Navigator. This SOS represented a first for this generation of MacLean's.

Tuck gathered his gear and made his way to his SUV for the forty-five minute drive to the launch site. As a reservist, he was technically always on call in a crisis situation, but contrary to popular belief, that seldom happened.

Family tradition demanded the MacLean men had to serve. You live by the sea and you know what's expected of you, that was their family motto. Tuck and Nate had spent a minimum of two years working Coast Guard. While Nate navigated, Tuck swam. He was strong, and powerfully built, and made for the sea. Billy was set to start his term when he turned twenty. At a time like this, Tuck was glad for family traditions.

The shoreline was being pounded raw, but that didn't matter when the people you loved were fighting for survival?

As Emily and the kids arrived, joining Tuck's mother, Daniel and Billy manned the radio on full alert, leaving Tuck to drive through the pounding rain to meet up with his Coast Guard crew.

*My family is out there, fighting for survival.*

Daniel's three oldest boys and a daughter, boys and girls no longer, but grown men and women with their own families, were out there.

The woman Tuck couldn't get out of his mind and heart was out there.

Did Vivian see his message when she sailed away?

Does she know what he meant when he touched his heart?

She owned his heart. Was it love? Tuck didn't know, but he wanted to find out. Could he really be in love after only a short period of time? *Yes!* He heaved a sigh as he drove.

The ego side of his being fleetingly hoped if he claimed her sexually, that would be that and he would resume life as he had before. But it wasn't that easy. Even as he watched the Navigator sail out of sight, with Vivian on it, all he wanted to do was jump on board to be with her.

There was no denying his true emotions. He had to get to her, to see her to safety. Vivian was now a part of him—his family, and his family was in trouble.

Tuck radioed his mother. "Dad's the best sailor, Ma. I'm sure he has everything in order. Nate's strong too. He's a good sailor. Everything will be okay."

"You be safe too," she whispered through the radio, sniffing away her distress.

Ending the call with his mother, he adjusted the frequency just in time to hear another call over his handheld. "Immediate assistance to the Navigator requested. Repeat, immediate assistance to the Navigator. Coordinates provided."

"Oh, God, no!" Tuck moaned, both hands gripping the wheel as he floored the SUV over the slippery road surface.

Who went over and for how long? Dear God, let them survive this raging storm.

Chapter Twelve

Instinctively, her arms reached out to flutter and create resistance against the drag of the water as she struggled toward the surface. Her eyes tried to focus on the receding grey light of the breaking water. *Calm, I must stay calm!*

The pressure of the water surrounding her weighed heavily against her head. She bent at the waist, reaching for her ankle. It was an almost unachievable task pushing through the wall of water. Vivian struggled with the bindings that held her firmly in their grasp. Images swam out of focus. Feeling lightheaded from the lack of air, she prayed for strength and fought for calm.

Her body convulsed and she straightened like an arrow ready for flight. She couldn't go anywhere, she was trapped and going down.

*Calm. Ohmigod, I'm not ready for this!*

Bending again, her fingers gripped the bindings, hoping for an escape. Just as she considered the situation helpless and all lost, something sharp sliced her finger. *The knife?* Nate had tossed it to her when she couldn't reach it, but she missed it, yet there— caught in the rope by the tip of the blade, was Nate's knife. Grappling for the handle with renewed vigor, Vivian began to saw loose of the bindings. She covered her mouth with one hand to prevent the natural instinct to suck in water in place of much-needed air. She had to work fast and didn't care if she cut her foot in the process.

More flashes of her life ran through her thoughts like a slide show. Unbidden, Vivian recalled the conversations she had had with Tuck about being a rescue swimmer. She had wondered what kind of bravery it took to voluntarily cast into the ranging ocean swells for the life of another.

Would he come for her? Will they find me?

She grew weaker. *I can't loosen my grip on this blade.* She convulsed again, her body wanting to give over and pull the water into her lungs. Moments mattered. Spots appeared before her eyes. *It is not over. I have to be strong. Someone will come for me.* But no one reached in and saved her from the raging sea. There was no one to rescue her from the black depths of the ocean. *I have to get free from this rope!*

With all the strength Vivian had left and as the final drops of oxygen ran through her lungs, she sawed the rope and finally floated upward. Giving over, she allowed the life jacket to buoy her to the surface, floating as in an ascent to heaven.

****

"One person recovered. One still missing. Coordinates to follow."

Tuck, in full survival gear, boarded the Hercules helicopter. "Dear Jesus, who?" he shouted to part of a three swimmer team.

Curt words flew between Tuck and the CO upon his arrival, to the effect that Tuck was too close to the victims. He was told he should sit this one out, but Tuck's record as an exceptional swimmer won the verbal battle.

"You need me," Tuck said with a firm voice. "You need all the help you can get in this storm! My family needs me and one way or another, I'm going."

*Vivian needs me.* He didn't need to be told. His heart sensed it was Vivian in the water. *I have to get to her. She needs me.*

He tried to project his thoughts to her. *I'm on my way, I'm coming for you, my love.*

\*\*\*\*

After what seemed like an eternity, Vivian's head broke free of the water. She had but a moment to sputter, barely able to draw in a new breath before she was under again. There was no time for coughing or gagging, or to rid her body of the unwelcomed salt water she had sucked into her lungs despite her best efforts. She would suck in more water than she already had. *I need air.*

When Vivian broke the surface once again, she was ready. She blew out hard and sucked in as much air as to fill her lungs before another wave struck. The waves tossed her like a seed in the wind. Rising out of the depths from which she just plunged, gigantic currents with the hand of a God would fist around her, taking her back down to the desolate darkness. Being physically strong did not determine survival.

The rain slicker over her life jacket was simply a hindrance at this point. Making it harder for her to break the surface, its billowy form sucked the weight of the water and pulled her further down when she needed to ride the surface. Vivian struggled out of the rain slicker while being tossed under the raging sea. Although the slicker was bright yellow, it covered her orange life jacket, which had a signal attached. *I have to pull the cord.* The signal would allow air rescue to see her despite the swelling seas. As she upended, her feet were tossed over her head and she somersaulted over the next break. *Please God, let someone come. Let someone see me. Let Tuck find me.*

On and on the waves slaughtered her body. She thought the misery would never end. Vivian had no notion of time. She couldn't even remember what time of day it had been when she first entered the writhing mass. Before dark? With the driving rain it was only a perception of the darkening sky. This did not intensify her fears as she had already been swallowed by the beast and was by this point beyond fear and numb with cold. Tired and exhausted, she still would not give in. If she were to survive she must stay awake. She forced her body to remain limp and flow with the water, rather than struggle and fight her way to the surface. Quickly adapting to the rhythm, she realized the waves had their own timing, and as each pull of the current sucked her down, the great hand of another wave tossed her back up.

Struggling to focus on something that would keep her alert, her only capable thought was Tuck. Those eyes, that easy smile, and the way he made love to her with passionate abandon. He was no passing fancy, she knew that from the start. He was also no holiday fling. Tuck was the real deal and she swore if she ever got out of this storm alive, she would take the chance necessary to make it work with him. She had been given something precious, and had to grab it and hold tight, doing whatever it took to keep it safe.

Breaking the surface with renewed flight, Vivian

let out a primal scream. *I will not be beat*. "I'm here!"
****

There it is, the Navigator. Tuck never imagined he would ever see one of the MacLean boats in this condition.

Another swell took the tall ship and listed it to the side as though she would capsize before righting again. The bow was completely submerged under the weight of the driving rain and water. The long vessel twisted, righted, and stood fast in her struggled. *You got it, Dad*.

"The expedition is on its way…over." Tuck's father's graveled voice filled his headpiece. "All hands save one accounted for…over."

"Do you require immediate evacuation? Over," the pilot asked.

"Negative. Evacuation not required. Can hold steady until the Expedition arrives. We are not taking on water in the hull. Repeat, ship sound except for loss of mast…over."

"Received. Will proceed to coordinates to search for sign of missing sailor. You have veered quite away from your original course. Confirm coordinates…over."

"Coordinates confirmed. Proceed…over."

"Will maintain radio contact…over." the pilot said.

"Affirmative…over." Tuck's father ended the transmission.

The Hercules flew through the driving rain like the great God for which it was named. When it reached the designated directions, it circled, falling right and veering, and steadying again. A dance in the ferocious clouds, man verses nature. Tuck was no fool to think that they had the upper hand.

The informative, unemotional voice of the co-pilot

filled his headset. "No sign of life," he reported. "Will continue to circle. Have enough fuel for three more runs then will have to return for refueling."

The three swimmers sat beside Tuck at the edge of the open helicopter door, searching for anything floating in the riling mass of foam. Nothing. Circle again. Nothing. *Goddamnit!* It can't be. Vivian had to be thrown off course as well. Tuck's practical mind contemplated the unthinkable. Just because she was tossed into the water at these coordinates doesn't mean the waves hadn't tossed her body further afield.

A crewman at head quarters would run the longitude and latitude and combine this information with the ocean current and wind direction to predict approximate location. All of this information was relayed by the multitude of ocean buoys. When the Hercules next took to the air, their destination would be adjusted according to the new figures.

Tuck prayed. *Please, let her be alive.*

The expedition arrived at the Navigator as the Hercules returned to base for fuel. Before Tuck had an opportunity to interject the departure, the pilot continued with finality. "We will return.

****

The storm represented a never ending nightmare, the rolling, the rocking, the twisting, and turning. Vivian would cry if she had the tears to spare. Fatigue and cold enveloped her. She could perceive a subtle difference to the pattern, a change in the momentum of the waves, but despite her best effort, she was succumbing to the tiredness. She was getting to let go when she heard a bell toll. *Wasn't that something I read somewhere?* Death was upon you when the bell tolled thrice?

Louder and insistent, the clanging penetrated the fog that consumed the present state of her brain.

Clang. As regular as the tossing of the ocean.

Clang. Two breaths.

Clang.

*Wait a minute!* Vivian mustered her waning strength to bob up higher in the water and glance around. She was no longer being dragged under consistently. She was actually bobbing, now riding the large swells.

Clang, clang, clang. What was that noise? Vivian couldn't seem to focus.

Clang, clang, clang. Has the bell tolled and she's in hell. Really, could this be it? She was no angel, but didn't think she'd head to hell for her transgressions. The clanging sounded again. There was something familiar about the sound. Something familiar penetrated. If only the fog would clear.

Clang, clang, clang.

*A buoy! Ohmigod, a buoy!* Vivian straightened and kicked her feet to stretch out of the water as much as she could, kicking with one last effort. *Where is it?* Her eyes were pasty from the salt water and the driving wind. She could barely open them but a slit to see a couple of feet in front of her.

Clang, clang, clang.

Was it getting closer or was she drifting away from it? She had to find it. It was her only salvation. Just then, to her right, a blurred object appeared. She kicked, moving in the direction of the sound. The sound grew marginally closer. Or was she imagining the whole thing? She couldn't be sure.

It seemed an endless struggle. Vivian's limbs wouldn't cooperate cold and numb as they were. Try as she might, she couldn't seem to scissor kick to the buoy. She had one shoe on while the other foot was bare. She pried the other shoe free with a final farewell for fashion in order to achieve better mobility, but she still wasn't making any headway. She grew eternally frightened that she would suddenly be flung away from the buoy by a rogue wave. Frustrated, Vivian splashed her arms in a forward motion, encumbered though they were by the bulkiness of the lifejacket, toward the sound.

Clang, clang, clang. The sound was getting closer. With renewed vigor, Vivian waded forward until she quite literally bumped into the buoy. The buoy was significantly bigger than she imagined. Somehow buoys, in the imagination of the masses, are small dots in the ocean, like markers on a map. But this buoy was larger than any good size SUV, if not a truck. More like a floating shed, except of course, she couldn't go inside. It seemed to be completely solid.

Ignoring the darkness of the night and the rain pelting down, Vivian ran her icy hands over the surface searching for a handhold. Relief warmed her that she was no longer being flung under the water, but she needed to stay connected with the buoy. For the first time since being deposited in the ocean, she grew more optimistic and alert by the moment. An adrenaline rush flowed through her veins, giving her renewed energy.

Legs in constant motion to keep her in place, Vivian continued to run her hands along the surface as she bobbed around the edge, searching for something, anything to hold on to. Panic made her strong. *I can't let the waves grab me and pull me under. I don't have the strength to go through that again.* Her mind registered on an old saying of when you were lost, stand still and someone would find you. This buoy would enable her to stop drifting and increase the chances of someone finding her.

Nate's lessons flashed through her mind, registering what she had considered meaningless information now quite significant. "A weather buoy is basically a weather station set strategically at sea to monitor currents, ocean temperatures, and wave heights," he had said as they reviewed the instruments on board the Navigator. "Scientists monitor these stations and report on an anomalies and weather changes. Anything and everything."

*If I can just get myself out of this freezing water, someone might find me.* Vivian continued to run her hands along the surface, feeling her way. She was sure there would be handholds, if not a ladder, and then suddenly she found it—a ladder.

Hoisting her soggy weight up the ladder took several attempts, each ending with her splashing back down into the cold depths, sputtering to the surface again and again. When she was finally up a couple of steps, she paused for breath. Vivian counted how many steps she had climbed, just to focus her mind. Six.

Would search and rescue be looking for her? If nothing else, they would search for her body. Would Tuck be on board? In a storm like this surely he would be called out. How devastating for him to have to his family in peril.

She hoped the crew on the Navigator had come through the worst of the storm? With Captain MacLean at the helm, she was sure they would.

Had Nate gotten out of the water? Yes, he had. She had to believe he did.

Would Tuck miss her if she was lost to the sea? There was something something special between her and Tuck. He touched his heart and waved as she left. He touched his heart. *I touched his heart.* Is that what he was saying through the gesture?

Clinging to latter, her life on the line, Vivian's very soul was stripped bare, leaving no room for pretense in her situation. She understood beyond a doubt that she had been given something rare with Tuck. That kind of connection had to be mutual, right? *It has to be.* The thought of Tuck gave her the will to keep hanging on as a wave threatened to disarm her from her present location. The wave passed and she hoisted up another step, agony traveling through the soles of her frozen bare feet to the top of her legs.

*Where are you, Tuck? I'm here. Please find me.*

The beacon attached to her lifejacket was long since lost with the battering of the water. Bitterness filled her as she glanced down at the place where the emergency light had been striving to cope. Even with the never-ending pain, she continued her climb. Reaching to top, she had found salvation. Now, she just needed someone to find her.

Vivian wrapped her icy fingertips around the ladder to lock her elbows so she encircled the contraption. She had to cope with her feet slipping, but she had a firm hold with her arms as she bent over the top of the clanging bell. Exhausted, she laid her head to rest in the hollow created by her arms. *Finally rest.*

Clang, clang, clang. The reverberating of the

clanging bell couldn't force her to keep her eyes open any longer. She dreamed of Tuck. They were on his small sloop making love, and enjoying the warm breeze and sunshine on their naked bodies. Her body registered heat, warmer than she had been since entering the cold ocean. She quaked with spasms of shivers, but her back *did* feel warm. Imagination was a wonderful thing. *Is this a result of hypothermia?*

She tried to lift her head, and then gave up. How long had she been out? She had no idea. Did it matter? *I'll just rest a bit longer.*

With all loss of time, her eyes fluttered again. She couldn't feel her arms. That couldn't be good. They were locked around the buoy's ladder. She eased her gripping fingers, flexing them to bring back a painful circulation. She tilted her head. The sun, high in the sky, warmed her skin as she continued to clutch the wide bars. Most of her body, except for her knees down, was fortunately out of the water. Vivian ached all over. The bars were digging into the cleft of her elbow were she held in a bear hug. *The sun feels good, but I'm parched.* Her tongue was glued to the roof of her mouth and her lips were caked with dried salt from the water. Easing her tongue out of her mouth, she could feel a wide crack in the middle of her bottom lip.

Cautiously, regaining sensation in her hand, she lifted her fingers to her face, to scratch the salty crust from her eyelashes. She glanced around her. The sea still roiled as though angry, but smoldered as the minutes passed. The ocean was vibrant in its overwhelming energy. The sky cleared with not a cloud to be seen directly overhead. She stared to the horizon. Her momentary elation of the surrounding beauty shattered as she peered to the distance where she saw the blue-grey of the storm approaching.

The buoy was a bright yellow with orange rings and metal surrounding the bell with a light at the top powered by solar energy. Dressed in beige pants, stretched and tattered, they hung off her slender hips. Her grey, wool sweater was soggy and covered by her orange lifejacket. Would she be visible to planes or helicopters searching for her? She had nothing, no flares to signal a rescue. *How can I possibly alert anyone I'm here?*

As light as the breeze was that blew over her, Vivian's whole body shook with tremors that started at the soles of her feet and worked their way up her entire body. Her tired brain tried to remember all she knew about hypothermia. Step one, conserve heat. She had to get out of the water. She brought her legs up to her chest to warm her core. With her legs out of the water, she lost her perilous balance atop of the buoy and before she could catch hold of a step, she fell back into the ocean. Expending energy she didn't have, and now freshly drenched, she dragged her body back to her perch.

*Damn!* So much for that. Dripping and colder than she had been before her dunk in the sea, she gazed to the horizon, becoming increasingly fearful of the approaching wall of terror.

Tentatively wiping the water out of her eyes with the tips of shaking fingers, Vivian noticed the sea begin to boil again. The waves lapping along the edge of the buoy were getting higher still. The water was rising. Rising fast! Where just moments ago only her knees were submerged, the waves now washed her back.

*Oh, God, no.* She prayed, seeing nothing but the vast expanse of ocean stretching forever in every direction. The wall of black closed in from all sides. *I really can't do this again.* Losing hope, Vivian hung her head toward her chest as great wracking sobs she didn't think she had the fortitude to produce, escaped her cracked and newly bleeding lips.

At first, she had mistakenly thought the storm approached from only one direction, but when realization dawned that she lay in the eye of the tempest, her faith shattered. The temporary respite was coming to an end. She had nothing to hold her to this buoy except the failing strength in her arms.

She lifted her head to glance around. *Think. There has to be something.* Her vision returned to the top of buoy.

As the first waves started to wash over her completely, setting the buoy lean this way and that, she was paralyzed. The current tipped the structure sideways, immersing her in the ocean and bobbing back up with the floating beacon. As the light at the top of buoy dipped into the sea, she accepted the waves that bathed her. *I know what I have to do.*

Chapter Thirteen

The Expedition found the Navigator and waited for the tug to arrive to assist the ship back to shore. Then the Expedition would join the search for Vivian. Three other ships had also sent out an SOS so the Coast Guard was busy.

Tuck's partner swimmers dove into the water. They rescued a sailor overboard, hanging on to pieces of his splintered fifteen-footer. The man tried to fight the rescue swimmer, which happened more often than not. People panicked as the cold shock of the water and fear overtook them. The sailor, being so frantic, he didn't know what he was doing. Tuck sat, ready to go into the water to help his comrade, but the swimmer had the situation well in hand as he turned the man in a standard head lock to save the sailor's life.

The next mission involved swimming to a trawler in distress, and ascertains that all souls were stable and waiting for a rescue ship. Tuck had to administer first aid to a deck hand and hoisted the man in the basket to return him safely to shore. A happy ending for all lives on board.

The Hercules then returned for refueling and set out again, all the while trying to locate Vivian. Tuck was beside himself with anxiety. *I can't stand the thought of her in that black barren water fighting for her life. I can't bear not finding her. What if I never see her again?* He simply would not consider not finding Vivian. She had to survive. He couldn't consider anything else.

Through the long night and into the day, the still hadn't found her. Tuck was becoming desperate. Convinced the coordinates his father had provided no longer applied, he gathered the charts. The Navigator had been thrown well off course with the hellish waves. It stood to reason a woman awash at sea would travel as far as a cork in raging, roiling water.

*I can't give up on her!* Tuck placed his head in his hands. *I won't!*

As twilight approached and the search had been ongoing for twenty-four hours, the possibility of finding Vivian alive diminished rapidly by every minute that passed.

\*\*\*\*

Clang, clang, clang.

*A weather buoy.* Vivian was surprised her brain still functioned.

When she first found the clanging beast, she remembered thinking it was a weather buoy, but dismissed the information as meaningless. For she had found salvation, however temporary, a weather buoy meant that someone, somewhere was monitoring the information sent by this big hunk of steel. In a storm like this, information matters. All buoys within the storm's circumference would be monitored to track the progress of the hurricane.

Vivian recalled Randy's add on lecture to Nate's explanation on the importance of buoys while navigating the sea. "The buoys out here measure air pressure, air temperature, sea surface temperature, wind observations, and the wave height."

The wave heights increased again. With nothing but the waning strength of her arms holding her to this buoy, she didn't think she would be able to survive the increasing persistency of the wave potency.

How in the hell had she even got into this trouble? Her longing for adventure, but this was not an adventure. This was life and death. Her life...or possibly her death in the next few hours as Vivian was convinced by the appearance of the wall of weather coming her way that she would not survive another few hours of bobbing in the sea, never mind the exposure, or lack of water.

She had to interfere with the signal the buoy was sending. The only way to capture anyone's attention was to interfere with the transmission of information. Someone wanted the information this big baby sends and if they didn't get it, they'd wonder why. With her heart in her throat, watching lightning dance along the wall of the eye, Vivian shimmied up the buoy's wire cage to the light and the housing protecting the mechanical workings of the machine. *This is where my experience with repairing old junk may come in handy.*

\*\*\*\*

The pilot walked toward Tuck with two steaming mugs of coffee. "Tuck, man," he said, handing him a cup. "I don't know. The eye is passing through and the other side seems worse than what we just went through."

"We never give up, man. Never."

"No, we don't give up, but we also don't chase lost causes in this shit. We don't unnecessarily risk more lives. People depend on us being there."

"She's out there. I can feel it." Tuck inspected the map again, striving to chart where in the ocean Vivian may be. A large, red X marked where the Navigator had been intercepted. There was another where Nate and Vivian went into the water. Tuck needed to factor in the direction of the wind and the waves to come to a hypothesis on where Vivian may have drifted over the course of the last twenty-four hours.

"Your own brother saw her go down with the mast and rigging. Nate said she was all caught up in the ropes. You and I both know that the likelihood of someone even surfacing after death is rare when a body is caught in the rigging. The way this sea is operating, Vivian is lost to us. I'm sorry to have to be the one to say it, man, she's gone."

*No!* Tuck wouldn't believe it. How could he tell the pilot that he could feel Vivian calling to him for help—that she was out there? They'd kick him off the squad and then where would he be? So he returned to his bench to sit resolute. As the pilot walked away, Tuck covered his face in his hands. How could I lose someone when I barely had time to understand she is the one? He lifted his face from his hands, tiling his head back to breathe deeply, staring at the florescent lights above. *I won't believe it. When she is gone, I will know and I know she isn't gone.* Not yet. Vivian was strong and he had to be strong for her.

Tears rolled down his face unashamed.

Physically exhausted from his recent missions of the last day, Tuck was mentally drained as well. The sea charts were rolled in his hands, held in a death grip as he fell into a fitful sleep on the bench, waiting for the next call to come through.

He pictured see her face. As soon as he closed his eyes, he could see her alight with the wonder of sailing his small sloop. Tuck marveled at the passion in her eyes, the expressions on her face clearly giving away her every emotion. She wore her heart on her sleeve as though she had never been schooled in the art of a poker face. Then his vision brought her to him and they were making love. Tuck smiled in his fitful sleep. As she drew him inside her, he gloried in being surrounded by her, and the fit of his body to hers. The seamless harmony of two bodies joined the way that they should.

He woke up with a start. "No!" Tuck scrubbed his hands over his face, the bristle of his unshaven face scratching across the palms of his hands. "You're not gone."

Tuck had never come this close to completeness before with a woman to lose it. One way or another he was heading back out there. He wouldn't stop until he had found her. He had to know one way or another, for as long as there was no sign, there would still be hope that she was out there…somewhere.

Tuck went back to the charting table to roll out to his maps, studying the readings, making notes of where Vivian and Nate went overboard, and where the Navigator was when the Expedition arrived. Using the information provided on their last run, he drew concentric circles around both sets of coordinates, plotted the areas they already searched, and the buoy locations. He would check with the Expedition's engineers to see what activity had been reported from the buoys within his search module to verify the storm's progress to decide where they would next concentrate their search efforts.

Naval officer, Innis, provided the information Tuck required when he pointed to one of the buoys he charted on his map.

"Buoy four-four-zero-one-one located at forty-one, point one degrees north, sixty-six, point six degrees west has no readings, sir." Innis pushed his glasses up his nose, his hand continuing to scratch his well messed hair.

"Nothing?" Tuck yawned, pulling his mind into full alert. Bending close to the screen to see better, he said. "What do you mean nothing?"

"Likely the storm caused some damage, sir. We'll notify Marine after the storm abates. They'll send a scientific crew out for repair."

"When did it last send signal?" Tuck body grew tense.

Innis paused, reading the monitor. "That's funny. This is unusual, sir." Innis tapped his screen as though willing the machinery to cooperate. "Up until just about an hour ago. I see here, by its position and the information we have from Marine, that it should now be dead center of the eye. Just like that, it has stopped sending signals. The last reporting had a maximum sustained winds of forty-nine knots with gusts to sixty-five knots and a significant wave height of thirty-nine fee, but that was just as the storm was abating in that area according to the satellite."

"You're saying it's not transmitting now?" Tuck ran both hands through his hair. "When it was in the eye? What would have thrown it out?"

"That's what's so weird, sir." Innis shook his head, tapping on the keyboard. "Last report shows pressure, wave height and temperature, and then nothing."

Freakish enough to mean something? That needle in the haystack to cause pause, and Tuck grabbed on for all it was worth. It was Vivian! She had told him that she loved to tinker with junk. She had to be responsible for this. It was worth investigating. She knows how things work, and she'd certainly know how to break something. What better signal than no signal at all?

"You're out of your mind, Tuck," said the CO. "You're grasping at straws."

"Be that as it may, it's worth checking into."

"That's one-hundred nautical miles from the drop location. Too far."

Tuck continued to argue. "Not too far given the size of those waves," he said, showing the CO his charts highlighting where the Navigator reported their first SOS. Then where they lost Nate and Vivian in the water, where they picked Nate up, where the Navigator was intercepted, and how far off course it had travelled. "Combine that with the two storms merging from different directions and the combination of the gulf current, I think this little buoy may have been a bit of salvation."

"Speaking of which, have you looked out the window? We're fixing for act two. People will need us and we have to be at the ready!"

"Vivian needs us!" Tuck stared at the CO. "We don't back down from a storm."

In the end Tuck exhausted his CO's patience, and got his way. One trip and one trip only.

\*\*\*\*

Vivian was tossed here and there, her legs banging against hard metal, cutting and bruising to the point she was sure one or both of her legs would break, if not already broken. She couldn't feel a thing.

She had her arms wrapped tight about the metal cage, locked at her wrists. Her face was pressed toward her chest, sheltering as much as she could from the frigid pellets of rain slashing her exposed skin. The lightning flashed around her, while the thunder screamed in her ears. Vivian could no longer watch the approach. It was like seeing the devil himself and she couldn't do it. Being surrounded and more frightened than she ever imagined, she hid her face in her arms. *Pray that I'll be found, that someone will notice the little buoy in the middle of nowhere suddenly not sending any signals.*

****

The Hercules dipped in the wind currents, falling freely until the rudders caught again, pulling the machine forward and up between the striking lightning and booming thunder.

They were circling the coordinates Tuck indicated. He couldn't see anything, including the buoy. The waves, like pockets of angry beasts, jumped clear of the ocean surface in an effort grab the craft and take it under.

His hands curled around the handles on either side of the door. "Lower," Tuck commanded. "We have to get lower."

Just then the helicopter took a sharp turn as they dropped in a cold air pocket, which threw them toward the sea. The pilot caught the gears and saved them, lifting them out from the drop. That's what the chopper was made for. Tuck breathed a sigh, returning to his scouting post. He turned back to the open door to scan the boiling surface. "There!" He released his grip on the handle to point. "Once more around. I see the buoy. Once more around."

"I can't hold it steady!"

"Yes you can. Once more, man. Please, once more to make sure."

Tuck focused through the driving rain to the bobbing and dipping buoy to see if anything was amiss. He jumped to his feet, arms braced to either side of the large chopper opening. "Ohmigod! It's her. I see Vivian!"

The incredulous pilot shook his head.

"I see her!" Tuck shouted as loud as he could. "I've got to go in." He rigged the harness before the pilot could disagree.

"On my mark," shouted the pilot. "Now!"

Tuck launched into the water, driving toward the clanging of the buoy. Waves washed over him, sinking him in its depths, but he kept pushing forward, the helicopter's searchlight illuminating his way.

He stopped to get his bearings. Bouncing with the waves, his breath literally left his body when he saw Vivian hanging on for dear life to the buoy as it dipped her in water. She appeared so small next to the buoy. She also seemed lifeless, but he didn't want to consider that now. *I have to get her back to the chopper, back to safety.*

It took Tuck several attempts to grab hold of the bars to hoist his body level with Vivian. He admired the strength it must have taken her to grab hold of the ladder in her condition and do what she had to do to simply survive.

Tuck reached for her leg and shouted her name. "Vivian!"

No response.

A wave sprang up to grab and toss him back into the roiling mess. He was able to launch out of the depths and back toward the buoy. Tuck clutched the steps of the ladder and climbed higher, squirming beside her, the searchlight illuminating them.

"Vivian!" He shouted over the howling of the wind and driving rain. "Vivian! Answer me!"

Taking his glove off, Tuck checked for a pulse at her neck and could barely feel life under the severely cold, blue tinged skin. Shouting into his radio transmitter, Tuck relayed that he would need the harness. "She's alive! Two souls coming aboard."

The pilot shouted back. "Only you, Tuck, would have such luck."

The helicopter dipped and strived to hold its course in the storm. Freeing Vivian's hands from the buoy proved troublesome as she had her wrists locked in a death grip. Her fingers were fastened so tightly he was fearful of breaking her bones.

"Time to go," Tuck whispered in her ear. "I've got you, Vivian. I've got you."

Chapter Fourteen

Vivian was drowning. Water washed into her mouth and nose, and she didn't bother to open her eyes any more. It was too much energy for her to care further. She had lost the battle, but didn't go down without a fight. *I went down fighting.*

Waves tossed her from side to side, and through the last midst of her struggle she thought she heard Tuck's voice in her ear. She would miss him. He was so easy to like and even easier to love. Amazing that after all this time, she could fall in love so quickly. Vivian thought it would take a while to love someone deeply. With Tuck, that wasn't true. She loved him from the moment he took hold of her shoulders. She had spent so much of her life searching for romance and love, only to find the right guy...and then lose him.

Cold, salty water ran down her throat and into her nose, choking her. She couldn't breathe. Vaguely she recalled some documentary she watched at one time that seemed to indicate it took six minutes to drown. *Surly it had been six minutes by now.* Not knowing how much longer she could endure the agony of being pulled apart by the pressure of the sea as it continued to batter and bruise her body, she surrendered. She sent a silent plea to whoever would listen to her prayers.

Tuck's voice was in her head again. She didn't want to go, but didn't have the strength to continue. *Let me go, Tuck. Let me go.*

"I've got you. Stay strong, baby, please. I need you." His voice was insistent in her ear, raspy as though fighting an emotional storm. "Stay with me! I've got you."

Perhaps the six minutes was the point to which the body stopped functioning, except your brain which lingered on and played your regrets and losses in slow motion one last time.

What would Saint Peter say when she met him at the gate? That she had given it her best shot, but between the cold and the water, no one was not strong enough to survive the storm.

She slipped. The water rushed over her head, swallowing her to the depths of the ocean as the strong currents took her. She was tossed like a rag doll. Vivian thought she was beyond feeling cold, but as the depths wrapped round her body, the ocean's temperature became even more frigid than before.

Then there was a jerk, a kick, and a tugging on her hair.

Her eyes quickly open.

Tuck's grey depths, housed in a clear plastic mask, greeted her under the water. His body tilted as he carried her out of the depths of the ocean and toward the surface.

****

He'd lost his grip. *Goddamnit.* Trying to stay in the troughs was hard enough in a boat, next to impossible as a swimmer, but he had to get there in order to get the harness attached. He grabbed the harness, but the helicopter jerked and a wave downed him, causing Vivian to slip from his grasp.

*Damn!* Tuck dove to retrieve her and missed. She was sinking unbelievably fast, her life jacket having slipped over her head when he grabbed her. Shooting for the surface, he used the same momentum to dive again and managed to grab hold of her hair as it haloed around her head. She would give him hell for that, but he had no choice.

As he hauled her upwards, face to face, he was rewarded for an instant when her eyes opened. His heart surged, giving him renewed strength.

"Tuck, man." The pilot's voice filled his earpiece as he broke the water's surface. "Okay, I see you. Get her in now. We're almost out of fuel and I can't hold steady. One shot. You've got one shot. Make it count!"

*One shot.* Tuck grabbed the harness again.

Holding on tightly to Vivian's unconscious form, he shouted. "I've got you, baby. Please stay with me!" Of all the thousand emotional currents running through him since spotting her holding on for her life, seeing her eyes open, if only for a second, put a lump in his throat. "Stay with me!"

\*\*\*\*

Tuck couldn't believe a woman who had been so vibrant just days earlier, would appear as fragile as she lay in the hospital bed.

Within another twenty-four hours, the storm had abated, finally. Another day had passed and Vivian still remained unconscious. The doctors were optimistic.

"Her body needs time." The attending nurses told him.

"She's been through a lot," the doctor said as Tuck sat beside her bed.

Her family had been notified, but they couldn't

come. The storm had basically washed out the airport. It would be a few more days before flights were back on track. So here he sat, relived to have his family back in port, and waiting, as he was, for those beautiful sea foam eyes to open. He held her hand, lying limp in his. *If only I have this one chance, I won't waste it.*

****

Vivian didn't want to open her eyes. She didn't know what she would see and she wasn't sure she wanted to see what lay in wait for her. Images of Tuck filter through her recovering mind. She wasn't surprised the he was the last thing she saw.

"I should have told you, Tuck. I should have told you I loved you." Regret colored Vivian's words and a tear leaked out the corner of her eyes.

"I love you too." When that easy going voice, deep with emotion answered her, Vivian's eyes fluttered open. An image of Tuck swam unfocused before her.

"Oh, no…Tuck…the storm…got you too." Her throat was raw and didn't seem to want to work. She coughed uncontrollably.

Vivian blinked. Confusion marred his beautiful gaze for a moment before clearing. Another male voice spoke close by.

"She's disorientated. Give her a moment to come around."

With much effort, Vivian widened her view by turning her pounding head to take in her surroundings. She ached all over. Tubes and dull grey walls surrounded her. No thunder, no waves, just beeps, hums, distant voices, and a man in a white lab coat.

Vivian registered a chuckle to her left and slowly swerved her head to gaze at Tuck.

At her frown, which he read like a book, Tuck reached down to cradle her face in his hands. "No, my love this is not funny. I am just happy to see your beautiful eyes again. I was so scared I would lose you before I even had a chance to tell you I love you."

"You found me," Vivian said in a barely audible whisper, searching his face, that handsome, strong face. "You really found me."

"Of course," Tuck said, leaning to stroke her bruised cheek, running his thumb lightly over the stitches above her left eye. His gaze was filled with love. "And mark my words, I have no intention of ever letting you go."

Vivian slowly reached up to touch his face, normally so easy going, now marred with lines of distress. "I love you, Tuck. I should have told you. I love you."

"I love you." His breath fanned her face as he bent to graze his lips over hers in the gentlest whisper of things to come.

## A word about the author...

*STORMS OF PASSION* is Lori Power's first published romance. She lives in St. Albert, Alberta with her husband and two sons.